NECROMANCER'S EMPATHY

Lily Clemons

Necromancer's Empathy by Lily Clemons[1]

Copyright © 2026 by Lily Clemons.

For more information:
www.authorlilyclemons.com

Book illustration by Sasha Ceart
Cover design by Steve Brite
Editor credit Brad Converse

ISBN - Paperback: 978-1-971908-00-7
ISBN - Hardcover : 978-1-971908-01-4
ISBN - eBook : 978-1-971908-02-1

First Edition: February 2026

---

[1] Lily Clemons (she/her)

Acknowledgements

I would like to extend a huge thank to the people who believed in me. From my son to my husband and of course my mother-in-law who was great at asking me 'how is the writing going?' just about every time I said hi to her.

I am very lucky to have incredibly supportive people in my life. My close friends who have supported this novel so much; Stephen Davison, Sasha Ceart, Eric Bush, Alyssa Sullivan, Dylan Larkin, Desiree Patten, Ozzy Rose, and Nicole Ndeto.

Thank you so much to my editor Brad Converse for helping me more than I can ever say. All the bazillion questions and clarifications I sent you! You might be a saint. I'm excited to work with you again!

Of course, I will be thanking Sasha Ceart and Steve Brite for the gorgeous art! Sasha for the cat and even more artwork on the website and Steve for creating such a gorgeous cover.

I would like to extend a huge thank you to the All Writers Online Workshop. They helped teach me so much about writing, pacing, and encouraged me every step of the way.

Chapter 1

I[2] had been googling how to raise human zombies. YouTube only got me so far, so Google it was. You'd think a necromancer would know how to raise people, but my specialty was a bit more specific than that. Namely, pets.

Being an intern at Undead, Inc., meant I could only ever bring dogs, gerbils, cats, etc. back to life. Never people. That's because you had to have a bachelor's degree in preternatural studies to get the higher-level cases. Until tonight. Thanks, Undead, Inc., for having staffing issues.

I bit my lip and tucked my brown hair behind my ear. I was going to do this. I had to do this. Mostly because Mrs. Bennett[3] was staring at me, *hard*.

Mrs. Bennett was a plump woman in a bright pink jumpsuit and designer tennis shoes. For some reason, she was wearing pearls and had on full makeup. She laid it on *thick*, which was the only reason I could see it at eleven at night.

Unlike her, I wasn't dressed up for the graveyard. Ripped jeans and a T-shirt suited me just fine, and there was no way I was going to wear makeup. This was a bloody job, so I strictly wore clothes I didn't care about. Which also meant I didn't exactly look professional to the client.

Nor to the coppas. Because of course, when you're raising a murder-victim from the dead, the cops would be around.

I stared down at the dead guy.[4] All I had to do was animate him, find out where Mrs. Bennett's missing cat was, and

---

[2] Lily Clarke (she/her)
[3] Mrs. Bennett (she/her)

then she would pay me enough to cover my rent for this month and last. This was probably why I was able to get the assignment. Undead, Inc., saw the words "pet cat" and assumed I'd be raising a cat. Nope. I was raising a guy who got himself killed last night.

He seemed old, maybe sixty. Even in the darkness, I noticed how ragged his skin was. I could tell he worked hard and was probably working on his last day too. With grey hair and laugh lines around his eyes, he could have been a super nice grandpa, at least if his throat hadn't been ripped out.

Mrs. Bennett had said he was her gardener, but I never knew that was such a dangerous gig.

"Please start promptly. I have an early appointment, and Aphrodite needs time to prepare for her party," Mrs. Bennett said. Her cat was having a party? I opened my mouth to ask and then thought better of it. I needed to bring this man to life; I couldn't get distracted by rich people being weird.

He had calloused hands folded over his stomach as he laid in what essentially looked like a hole. It was like the police thought they needed to dump a body in a ditch for him to be raisable. He was still wearing the clothes he died in, overalls covered in blood, and his work boots were still on.

I grimaced; he smelled like sweetbreads I'd buy from the butcher. Dead bodies didn't stink until a couple days passed. After that, the gases inside the corpse would release and smell absolutely foul. I knelt beside him and glanced at the cat carrier next to me, where a chicken was sleeping. An exchange had to be made with any kind of magic, and necromancy was definitely a form of magic. In this case, it was a life for a life. Normally if I bled a mouse,

---

[4] Ricky Baun (he/him)

it was enough blood to raise just about any animal from the dead. A mouse was gonna be nowhere near enough for a person.

I turned and slowly opened the carrier. I pulled out the chicken gently and tried to breathe through my mouth instead of my nose.

"Oh, my Gods, are you going to kill it?!" Mrs. Bennett gasped. I pressed my lips tightly together. Yeah, this wasn't gonna be good. YouTube had shown me how to do this earlier, but seeing it and doing it were completely different. The chicken flapped its wings and struggled in my grip. It must have felt my hands shaking.

I took a deep breath. Just needed to break the neck. I felt the crack of bones, but the legs were still moving. I screamed and dropped the chicken to the ground as it continued to flail.

"It's dead, why are you screaming?" the detective[5] asked. I was several feet away at this point and trying to remember how breathing worked. My hands were trembling as I watched the bird twitch on the ground.

"It still moves after it dies?!" I asked in horror. He rolled his eyes at me.

The detective was tall and lean. His khaki skin tone with a touch of stubble made him look gorgeous. He had thick black hair and deep hazel eyes. Earlier, he said he was a second-generation American from India. He specialized in homicide, missing people, and in the killing of chickens, apparently.

He had two officers with him, a tall Asian man and a young white woman. They were expressionless, except when I

---

[5] Detective Malik Sule (he/him)

7

dropped the bird. That got a smile or two. They were back to being expressionless now though. Okay, no big deal. I just had four people watching me. Google implied I could do this with some chicken blood and graveyard dirt. I cut into the chicken and grimaced as I felt the hot sensation of blood dripping onto my legs. I should have done this hunched over. Ugh.

I sprinkled the blood onto the makeshift grave and flicked it over the dead guy's face. Almost immediately, a cool sensation covered me.

Necromancy wasn't common. Less than one percent of the global population was able to do it. And yet, here I was. A necromancer intern attempting to raise my first human body.

An unnatural wind blew around me, then a haunting chill, and I could feel him. I closed my eyes and reached out my hands. Online it said necromancers could make two kinds of zombies: One was the decaying corpse, which was super gross, and the other looked like the person could be alive. I hoped I could do the latter. The former might make me throw up.

I wasn't touching him, but I could still feel his body pull itself together. His throat, which was ripped out, was repairing itself temporarily. Thank Gods.

I opened my eyes and looked into his grey ones. He smelled like sweat and fertilizer, which was way better than butcher meat. He looked like he could be alive. Some of the corpses I saw on YouTube looked like they were rotting, but he seemed fine. My body was thrumming from what I just did. I was cold to the bone and still vibrating with power. It was like a high as the dizziness gave me a pleasant buzz.

He stared at me, and I stared back. It was such an odd feeling. I was looking at a person that I brought back to life.

He was *mine,* and he would do anything I wanted. I scrambled backward and wiped my hands aggressively over my jeans, trying to get rid of the sensation of fresh blood. Mice didn't feel so heavy. It didn't feel like death. My trance was broken by the sound of the female officer throwing up while the Asian one held back her hair and looked at me.

"Did she really just raise that guy?!" He stammered. Mrs. Bennett had her arms crossed and was tapping her foot impatiently. I guess she wasn't impressed by the raising.

"Yes, officers. This is what it looks like when a corpse is reanimated for interrogation," Malik stated plainly to his coworkers and then turned to me. "Is it ready to be questioned?" The detective asked.

It? The man in the ditch didn't seem like an *it* to me. The gardener slowly moved to get out of the hole. He was at an awkward angle, with his legs higher than his head. What on earth were the cops thinking when they dumped him in there? I reached out my hand to help him as his stress washed over me. He felt scared, but his face was stone-cold. What made me think he was scared? No. I *knew* he was scared. There was no thinking about it. He was my zombie, and he was scared.

"Give him a second," I demanded as I helped him to his feet. "You okay?" I asked the zombie quietly.

"Thank ya, ma'am," he said in a soft gravelly voice. He sounded like I thought he would. A Southern gentleman.

"You ready to talk to the detective?" I continued.

He nodded his head at me.

Zombies could only be "alive" for an hour, so we didn't have a ton of time. After an hour, they began decomposing and couldn't be raised again. If he was put back in less than an hour, his family could still raise him later to say goodbye. I glanced at the time: 11:18 p.m. The clock was ticking.

"My name is Detective Malik," the detective said without wasting any time. "I am going to ask you a few questions, and then you can speak with your previous employer over there." He motioned to the two officers. The woman was kneeling on the ground, looking anywhere but at us, but the Asian man nodded and said something to Mrs. Bennett. She huffed, then followed him away from the scene. I guess she wasn't privy to the murder investigation. Did that make me special?

The gardener wiped the dirt off his clothes and didn't seem to hear Malik. It wasn't until I nudged him that he went to full attention.

"What d'you wanna know?" the zombie asked with a Southern drawl. I couldn't help but smile. He was definitely grandpa material. He just seemed so wholesome when he didn't have his throat ripped out.

"Are you Ricky Baun?" the detective asked, his tone cold.

"Yeah, that's me."

"Did you work with David Colt?"[6]

"Yeah, we both did the landscaping for the missus."

"What happened last night?"

Unlike the other questions he seemed to answer without thought, Ricky paused and seemed to really consider the question. There was a lot of debate on whether zombies

_____

[6] David Colt (he/him)

10

were capable of thought, but I knew he was thinking. He could think, he could feel, and here he was trying to remember what happened. In this moment, my zombie was a person.

"Me and Dave were doing some last-minute plantin' fer the tea party when a guy[7] showed up. He seemed mad that Dave and I were workin' together. He said vamps and people shoulden do that. He said he should kill us. I reckon he did," Ricky said and motioned to the shallow grave he was standing by. "I'm guessin' Dave dead too?"

Detective Malik nodded, zero emotion on his face. Necromancers couldn't raise vampires from the dead, so Dave's story was up to Ricky to tell.

"The vampire, David Colt, was burned to ashes. We identified him by his metal name tag. Now, let's return to the actual crime," Malik said shortly. It was obvious he wasn't as concerned about the death of a vampire. Why would he be? Vampire rights were still a new thing. Even if David was a person, ashes weren't raisable anyway. Ricky was the *actual* crime; David was just an undead thing that was now fully dead. I hated that.

Ricky reached out for my hand, and I intertwined our fingers. He was older than me, and his hand felt so strong and sure. Yet, he was clinging to me. It was such a childlike gesture on his part, and I felt like I had to reassure him. I squeezed his hand and gave him a small smile. He wasn't alone.

"Why did the attacker get mad that you and the vampire were working together?"

"He said vamps and people just didn't belong together. Predator and food. Nonsense thinkin', that's what that was.

_____

[7] To be Revealed (he/him)

Then he flashed his fangs and charged at us." He looked at me, and I guess my eyes gave away my shock at his callous way of talking about his murder. "Don't worry, I died quick enough," he assured me. He shouldn't have been the one comforting me, but I took it anyway.

"The killer was a vampire?"

"Yeah."

"It was only one individual?"

"Yup."

"What did the killer look like? Did you know him?"

Ricky paused and pressed closer to me. "Tall with a bunch of squiggly tattoos all over. He coulda been white or somethin' else. Hard to tell with all the squiggles. Black hair and black eyes too." He stopped and turned to me. "This ain't a dream, is it? I really died."

Pets never asked that. When I animated a cat or bunny, they were just happy to see their owner. They never asked if they were dead. Would it be impeding the investigation if I told him the truth? I glanced at Detective Malik, but he was just staring at me as though I was the one holding up the investigation, not the zombie.

"You died yesterday," I said and watched his face crumble. If he could cry, I knew he would have.

"Did David know the vampire that killed you both?" Malik asked, unphased by the life-or-death drama.

"He seemed just as surprised as me. Said he wasn' involved in politic stuff, but the vamp didn' seem to care. He didn' say much else. He was gonna kill just Dave, but I tried to fight 'im off. Stupid, really. I'm just human. But we had been workin' together for a long time. Made sense to try," he explained. "Can I call my wife? She's gon' be worried about me. My son too. He's off in Washington but is suppos' to come back home for the holidays," Ricky said. The detective closed his notepad and turned to me. I guess I was the one who had to keep breaking the news.

I glanced at my phone. It was 12:10 a.m. We were running out of time.

"I'm sorry, but we can't do that," I said and squeezed his hand. The phone call would probably make things worse. Plus, I wasn't allowed to let zombies interact with people outside of the client. Company policy.

The longest I'd reanimated anything was an hour and a half. I quickly learned the reason why that wasn't allowed: Zombies fell apart so quickly after that. The energy it took to raise the dead sped up the decaying process. This bit I learned from college rather than the internet. If school wasn't so expensive, I'd have a bachelor's in preternatural studies and be more than just an intern necromancer. Even though necromancy was rare, politics was still a thing. That expensive piece of paper separated the pros from the interns.

Ricky's hands were trembling as he pressed his lips tightly together. I had to lay him to rest before the time, otherwise his family would never be able to raise him again.

"Your client is free to question him now," Malik said and motioned to his partner to allow Mrs. Bennett to come over. She nearly tripped in her rush to get to us.

"Ricky, where is my Aphrodite?!" She demanded. The gardener no longer held my hand as he scowled at her.

"I dropped her off at the groomer like I always do on Tuesdays," he said impatiently.

"But they said she's not there," Mrs. Bennett's voice raised into a squeal. "Didn't you pick her up?!"

"No. I was busy dyin' and that dumb cat's not my problem no more." The defiance on his face made me smile. What did she expect from a dead guy? It's not like he was going to work tomorrow.

Mrs. Bennett let out a screech of agitation, then turned to me. "Will you be willing to continue the search for her? I'll pay you double."

Well, yeah. I'd learn how to find a missing cat for four months' rent. How hard could it be?

"What about the police?" I asked her and tilted my head in confusion. She just scoffed.

"They didn't even check the groomer's and barely let me talk to dear Ritchy." She stifled a sob but couldn't even remember her dead employee's actual name. With a murder investigation going, it made sense why a cat wouldn't be a priority. Plus, I could *definitely* use the money. I nodded with a grin. I could figure out how to detective my way to rent.

"My assistant will call you with additional details shortly. We already spoke to the groomer, but we had assumed she had been picked up by Ritchy. Apparently not," she said and turned on her heel to leave. "This has been a waste of my time. I can't believe I had to come to a graveyard in the middle of the night..." Her words became less audible the further away she got. I shook my head. She didn't give two shits that her gardeners were dead.

Ricky was giving me wide eyes like he knew what would happen next. I tried to give him a comforting smile. It didn't seem to work. "Please, can I stay?" he asked softly. I took his face in my hands and kissed his forehead.

I wanted to ignore the consequences. But maybe Ricky could be different. He'd go see his family, say goodbye, and finally move on. I knew I couldn't do that. It'd be worse if I ruined his chances of ever coming back.

Instead, I looked at the man in front of me and let him die. It was as simple as it was for animals. Like releasing a breath I'd been holding. His injuries returned, the life left his eyes, and he smelled like any other decaying corpse, somewhat sweet and full of regret. My eyes burned as I watched him fall to the ground in a crumpled heap, the life completely gone. I wiped away my tears.

I turned around and saw the chicken. I had no idea how the waste disposal of bigger worked. Mice were simple, there was always a compost bin on site, but a chicken? It was another thing Google forgot to mention.

Just when I was debating whether to look for the caretaker, I noticed the detective staring at me.

"Where did you learn necromancy from?" Detective Malik asked, making me jump. He had his arms crossed over his chest and was looking at me so intensely that I floundered to come up with a response that didn't sound stupid. I mean, how do you tell a cop you googled how to do your job and this was your first human raising?

"Well, I'm an intern at Undead, Inc.," I said nervously and ran a hand through my hair as I tried to look anywhere else but at him.

I wasn't sure if I should be offering my two cents, but I glanced back over at the makeshift grave and my stomach twisted. "By the way, the corpse doesn't need to be buried to be raised," I said so that the next zombie wouldn't have to crawl out of a grave. "Raisings don't even have to be at night either."

He pulled out his notepad from earlier and scribbled something down. "We have hired people from Undead, Inc., before, but you're the first person to say this. We are always told to have the dead at a graveyard and for the sun to be down. You know more than them," he said, his eyes so focused that it felt like he was looking into my soul. It almost sounded like he was suspicious of me. What did I do?

I thought my first human raising went pretty well. I brought the guy to life, he didn't look like a corpse, he could talk, and I was able to put him back into the ground. Granted, I totally cried there at the end, but most likely I'd toughen up over time.

"The professionals at Undead, Inc., are better than me. They've got the degree to prove it." Without a bachelor's degree, a necromancer can't be more than an intern at Undead, Inc. There's no way someone like me, with almost no formal education, could be better than the full-timers at my company.

"Your name is Lily Clarke, correct?" Detective Malik asked with his pen ready. I swallowed hard. It felt like he was going to report me. For what? Being too good for a novice?

"That's my name, don't wear it out," I said with a forced smile. He nodded, then turned around.

"You're done with that thing?" The female cop asked with a slight nod toward me. Wait. Was I the thing?

"I finished with the necromancer," he said, emphasizing the final word, then motioned to the chicken.

"Oh, right!" What do I do with leftover chicken? "Do you think y'all could take care of the bird?"

"I'll make my team a meal tonight," he said. Although it sounded like he was serious by his tone, I could see a slight upturn to his lips, and there was a slight glint to his eyes. He was teasing me!

"You do that, then," I scoffed and stormed off to my car. As soon as I was far enough away from the corpse, my body seemed to crash. It felt like I was forcing myself through a wall of molasses. The dizziness from before reached new heights as I tried to keep myself steady. I glanced at my phone and got the notification that I was just paid. Pet case means twenty bucks. Do I tell them it was actually a human? Or would I get in trouble for doing the job despite not being qualified. I sighed. Screw it. Twenty bucks for my first human raising. I barely managed to make it to my dumpster pile of a car before I got a phone call.

It was Mrs. Bennett's assistant. She gave me the groomer's address, as well as several pictures of Mrs. Bennett's darling cat, Aphrodite, who was suddenly worth $2,000.

Chapter 2

I was much more comfortable around graveyards than in downtown Dallas. First of all, parking was way easier at graveyards, especially at night. No need for parking meters, one-ways, or people who couldn't parallel park but tried to anyway. Plus, dead people in the dirt were way easier to manage than alive people in the city.

The groomer's wasn't too far from my apartment, which meant I was that much closer to my bed. I'd raised an actual human tonight! Exciting, sure, but my body was absolutely drained. If I had money, I would have taken an Uber home. Who knew bringing people back to life would be so exhausting?

I crawled out of my car through the passenger side door and grimaced as the handle tried to fall off again. At some point, I was going to fix my car, but that'd be after I paid rent and maybe bought groceries. Groceries sounded good. It implied food, and I hadn't eaten anything much in a week.

The Paw Lounge. I thought the name was cute when it was texted to me, but looking at the building, it was way more obnoxious than I could have imagined. The outside looked like a spa, like one of those fancy ones that was basically a resort. There was a doorbell to call for a concierge if you needed help with your pet's luggage. I guess it doubled as a pet hotel? The outside building was a light tan with a tinge of pink, and the windows had thick velvet curtains behind the glass. It looked like just the kind of place Mrs. Bennett would bring her cat to.

I looked down at my dark sweater and hoped it didn't smell like chicken blood. I probably looked like somebody's lackey. I wanted to get this over with, so even though my hair was a wreck and my clothes probably had graveyard residue, I still needed to walk into this pompous place and find the cat. Or at least some kind of hint as to who catnapped her.

As I walked up to the doors, I noticed two vampires off to the side talking. My friends could never tell a vampire from a human, but to me, it seemed obvious. Vampires just felt cold. It's similar to the dead I raised, but there was a hint of warmth to them. That must be from the blood. Maybe if zombies drank blood or ate brains, they'd feel more alive too.

The taller of the two had a poodle in his[8] arms, which he frequently stroked as he spoke quietly with the man in front of him. Not all vampires looked pretty. Most of the ones I'd seen just looked like pale versions of humans, but these two were very pretty. The one with the dog had long grey hair, which was straight and shiny even from this distance. He had thick full lips and defined cheekbones. With how slim he was and how he carried himself, I wouldn't have been surprised if he turned out to be a model. Undead models were becoming more and more popular lately.

The shorter[9] one was even cuter. He had to have been about my height, which meant short. But he had blond hair that went down to his shoulders. Although his hair was also straight, there was a hint of a wave to it. As I walked closer to the groomer's, it was clear how intensely purple his eyes

---

[8] Carmillo (he/they)
[9] Hale (he/him)

were. I didn't think vampires could have such unnatural eye colors. His face was a bit round, almost boyish, but overall, he reminded me of a prince from the countless Disney movies I'd seen. Definitely too pretty for someone like me. He glanced over at me and smiled. I don't know what expression I made, but he began to laugh. It was melodic and somehow scripted, like he was playing the part of a cute boy getting noticed.

Whatever. I felt insulted. Like he expected chubby girls like me to fawn over him and found it amusing that he caught sight of another one. Well, he didn't raise a murder victim from the grave tonight! As soon as I entered the building, I was hit by the smell of chamomile. It was super super strong. I already hated that odor, so to be suffocated by it was one of the worst ways to die.

"Good evening, are you here for pickup?" the lady[10] at the front desk asked, barely managing to hide her disapproval. She did not seem amused as I coughed repeatedly, trying to get the taste of chamomile perfume out of my mouth. Was this place trying to kill people?

I looked up at her and wasn't surprised by her appearance. She had on pearl earrings and a white blouse, and although I couldn't tell for certain, her forced pleasantries made me think she wore pantyhose. I shook my head in response to her question and pressed closer to the counter. No one else seemed to be in the building. With the dim lighting and the lack of groomers, I assumed most of the pets were sleeping. It was 3 a.m., so that made sense. It was becoming more common for places to stay open this late, mostly because the undead needed to get their errands done too, and

---

[10] Patty (she/her)

during the day, they had that whole "bursting into flames" issue.

"A woman named Mrs. Bennett brings her cat here all the time. Can you tell me the date and the name of the person who last picked up Aphrodite?" I asked, trying to be pleasant and professional. The smell was starting to make me lightheaded. The lady squinted at me. She was going to make things difficult, I could tell.

"I'll have to check with the client to see if I'm allowed to give out that information," she said shortly and picked up the phone. She was dialing without having to look anything up. Maybe Mrs. Bennett had been coming here for a long time. "Your name?" she asked, her tone still short. I noticed her name tag said Patty. Hilarious that even a pretentious place like this used name tags.

"Lily Clarke," I said and stuffed my hands in my pockets while I rested my hip against the counter. Seemed like I was going to be here for a minute.

Her conversation with whoever answered the phone was brief, but I could tell by the voice that it wasn't Mrs. Bennett, probably her assistant or butler. She had mentioned something before about having a butler. When Patty turned to me, her entire demeanor changed. She even smiled one of those fake customer service smiles at me.

"I'll pull up the information now, Ms. Clarke," she said.

While she was staring at her computer, a man entered behind me. It was the vampire from outside with his dog. I could see a hint of his fangs as he cooed at his poodle. His dog seemed excited from the attention and gave a soft yip as though he was conversing. It was sickeningly cute.

Patty gave him a genuine smile. "I'll be right with you, sir," she said, obviously more excited for him than me. "A man named Sebastian[11] came two nights ago around this same time," she said with a happy look on her face, as though she was finally about to be rid of me. I normally wouldn't have bothered, but I was feeling petty. So, I figured I should be the one to break the news to "Patty."

"Sebastian kidnapped the cat. He wasn't authorized to have access to her," I said, causing her eyes to widen. She quickly lowered her voice, not that it would do much good since the vampire would still be able to hear her. Vampire super-hearing and all that jazz. He was no longer talking to his dog.

"I will find out who released the pet to make sure they never do it without checking with the client. This should never have happened," she said solemnly, but it was obvious she was just trying to save her ass. I knew then that she was probably the assistant manager or manager. Regular employees wouldn't care this much.

"You gonna call the police too?" I asked with a raised eyebrow. I wasn't entirely certain how quickly the police would get involved, but this did seem more up their alley than mine. Plus, I liked seeing Patty squirm.

"Of course," she said and smiled, showing all of her teeth in the process.

"I'll let Mrs. Bennett know about the negligence of this facility. We will be in touch," I said in an attempt to sound like I had some kind of authority in the matter when I very much did not. Granted, Mrs. Bennett probably would be pissed about this in her pompous rich lady way. I could see

---

[11] Sebastian (he/him)

her taking her business, as well as the business of all her lovely rich friends, to a different establishment. I had no doubt the next groomers would be just as gaudy, if not gaudier. Who knew? Maybe it wouldn't smell like chamomile.

I messaged Mrs. Bennett's assistant to let her know the cat was picked up by someone named Sebastian. I figured my gig ended there, but in less than a minute, I received a reply saying that they'll double the pay if I keep searching. Great. Was I a private investigator now? How do you even track someone down with just a single name? Not even a surname! I held my phone a bit tighter in my hand. I got this. Probably.

Chapter 3

Gods, I just wanted my bed. This was turning out to be way longer of a day than I intended, but hey, I got a job for over $4,000 which is definitely a pretty penny. A couple more than a penny, but who's counting? Me. I'm definitely counting.

Outside, there was a chill in the air. Kind of funny given how humid it was earlier, but I guess that's what living in Texas is like. I rubbed my arms and walked quickly down the sidewalk. During the day, this section of downtown was usually bustling with people. But tonight, there was just darkness. I walked quickly and tried to ignore the feeling of being followed.

When I made it to the intersection, I glanced both ways, but before I could cross, I was forcibly grabbed from behind.

"Whoa! Hi there," I said quickly and looked behind me. It was a guy who had to be over six feet. He was grimy and had dark matted hair over his eyes. He leaned so close to me that I could practically taste the alcohol coming off him. This wasn't the safest area at night. I knew that. Why was I so stupid?! I should never have come here after the graveyard.

"It's not safe alone," he slurred. Well, duh. He was definitely part of the unsafe crowd. I looked him over the best I could with him behind me and couldn't see a weapon. Thank Gods.

"I'm almost to my car, so no worries," I said and tried to pull away from him, but his hand gripped my arm tighter.

"It's not safe," he repeated and leaned in while grabbing me tighter. I forced myself to the ground to try to surprise him into letting me go. He didn't. His grip tightened, and I gasped in pain.

"I think you're the one who isn't safe," a voice said and gripped his wrist. It was the short vampire from earlier. He still had that Prince Charming smile. I watched the vampire's eyes flash momentarily, and then the drunk man willingly let me go. "You should leave," he ordered.

"Yeah, I should," the drunk man nodded, his eyes clouding over as he stumbled away. For a moment, I thought the vampire thralled him, but that was illegal.

"Thanks," I breathed as I forced myself to my feet. He reached out for my hand, and I gladly took it. I was still a little off from the necromancy earlier. Humans were too much. I probably shouldn't do it again at this rate.

"Are you hurt?"

I shook my head.

"Where to?" He asked while continuing to hold my hand. His scent embraced me, a mix of lavender and lemongrass. I wanted to lean against him and pretend for a moment that I had a hot and cool boyfriend. My self-esteem wasn't terrible, but I was a plus-sized girl. I knew my worth. It had to be obvious to anyone walking by that we weren't dating. A girl could dream though.

"My pleasure," he said with a soft smile. I'd never spent so much time with a guy my height before. It was nice not looking up at someone, and he was just so pretty. I instinctively let go of his hand and crossed my arms to cover my stomach. I wasn't exactly slim, especially not like him. I had mousy short brown hair and big brown eyes, and although I definitely had curves, which included a stomach and thick arms, I wasn't the kind of girl who would normally be seen around a guy like this.

"My name is Hale, what's yours?" He slowed his pace, making me slow mine too. Was he trying to draw this out? Why? I stuffed my hands in my pockets and pretended not to check him out.

"I'm Lily."

"So, what are you doing out so late at night?" He continued, his body pressing closer to mine as we walked so our arms occasionally bumped. Was he flirting? I pressed my lips tighter together as I tried to think of what to do. Should I just... flirt back?

"I'm figuring out my life," I explained, deciding I might as well give him the truth. Hale grinned and brushed his hair back from his face.

"Figuring out your life, huh? How's that going?" He sounded way too amused, which only made me smile too.

"A bit better today than yesterday, but maybe a little worse too," I admitted with a sheepish smile. He grinned.

"Sounds wonderfully complicated."

"You have no idea."

He paused briefly and looked up at the sky. We couldn't see the stars in the city, just a light haze over the darkness. Even so, I looked up too. Sometimes people say the vastness of the sky reminds them how small they are. For me, it just wasn't true. When I looked up at the sky, I felt a little less alone. After all, how many other people were looking up at this same sky right now?

"Maybe I could do with a little 'figuring out my life' right about now," Hale spoke the words so softly I almost didn't catch them. But then I saw my car. It was a stark reminder that Hale and I were from different worlds. While he was Prince Charming, I was...

"My car is over there," I stumbled over my words as I motioned to the dingiest car on the street. It was covered in dents, had chipped paint, and the bumper was dangerously loose. It wasn't the kind of car I'd admit to owning, but for some reason, I needed him to understand just how below his league I really was. Sure enough, he grimaced, and I felt an odd sense of relief. I didn't want any false hope when it came to him.

"Is that thing even legal?" Hale asked, which made me laugh. I didn't expect him to be so blunt.

"It passed inspection," I shrugged, my smile too wide. Of course, I had to bribe the mechanic. It was one of those mechanic shops that changed ownership on the regular for tax fraud. Granted, he made my registration current, so who was I to judge?

"Barely, I'm sure," Hale scoffed, then rested his cold hand on my cheek. It forced me to look at his face. "Why are you so dangerous?"

What did he mean? How was someone like *me* dangerous? I wanted to read his mind to figure out what on earth his deal was. I didn't possess psychic abilities, but I was a girl alone with a guy. I wanted to know if he realized how this looked. Unlike me with the drunkard, this could be something.

28

His lips were light pink and thin and absolutely kissable. I backed away, making him drop his hand.

"I should get going," I said and opened the passenger-side door. The driver's side door didn't work anymore, which meant I always had to climb in through the other side. It wasn't the most graceful, but I couldn't afford to fix it. This cat would turn things around though. I'd be able to pay rent, buy groceries, and spin the wheel to see what I could fix on my car. Not literally, because the power steering was going out, but still.

"Has anyone ever told you that you make people feel the need to take care of you?" He asked with a raised eyebrow. I hesitated and tried not to feel insulted, but it was too late. Yeah, I needed help sometimes, but I didn't think that made me any less independent. The thing with the drunk guy was a fluke. It's not like I was asking for handouts. I didn't even ask for Hale's help to begin with.

"I wasn't trying to upset you," he spoke quietly. I blinked hard. Yeah, my eyes were watering. When did that happen? Was it just that long of a night? I was just tired. Too tired, too overwhelmed, and absolutely starved. I probably still had some iced coffee left over in the fridge at home. That would tide me over for a bit.

"I'm sorry," Hale said and reached out towards me. I flinched, which made him freeze. "Can I make it up to you? I thought this was going well until I messed it up." He knelt beside my door. I looked at him and wanted to believe his sincerity, but really, I just needed my bed. If I could get some sleep and recharge after all this craziness, then I'd be fine. Maybe I was just hangry. Even though I left the groomer's, I still felt lightheaded, which meant it wasn't just the chamomile.

"I need my bed and some food, nothing to do with you," I said with a shrug and blinked hard to get rid of the waterworks. "You should get going if you don't want to fill an ashtray." He gave me an apologetic smile and kissed my forehead.

"I'll make it up to you later, Lily. I hope I can see you again soon," he said and left. I watched him go for a few moments, then moved the rest of the way into the driver's seat. The spot where he kissed me tingled, a cold sensation, but I was quickly heating up from embarrassment. Did a guy seriously just kiss me? There was no reason to get so excited about it. I needed to get home and sleep. No way I'd see that guy ever again.

Even though I wanted to.

Chapter 4

I woke up to my phone ringing. Normally, that meant my mother[12] or a collection company. I really hoped it was the latter. My body didn't want to move, but I reached over to my dresser and grabbed the offending noise. My black cat, Mint, swatted at me for daring to adjust my body while she slept on me, but I ignored her snarky ass.

When I picked up my phone, I realized I was wrong. Undead, Inc., didn't call interns. The only phone call I ever got was an automated message saying I was hired. Since they were calling, then that meant I'd fucked up. Damn. Either the detective or Mrs. Bennett was getting me fired. Somehow the company must have found out it was my first human raising. I didn't technically lie to them when I agreed to take the case. But it was totally omission. I answered the phone.

"This is Lily," my voice cracked. I should have sipped water first.

"Good afternoon, Lily. This is Peter,[13] a receptionist at Undead, Inc. Is now a good time," he said, rather than asked. It didn't sound like I'd get another chance if I said no.

"Yeah, whatcha need?" I grabbed a bottle of stale water from the floor by my bed. I started chugging.

"The Preternatural Investigation Unit of North Texas has requested you work for them," he said. I choked. Hard. I mean, what was I supposed to do? Me? Getting asked to work with the police? This had to be a joke. Peter had the

---

[12] Mother (she/her)
[13] Peter (he/him)

decency to wait until I got my breath back. "However, as an intern, this is unprecedented. You will need to undergo a series of tests to make sure you are qualified to represent the company. I will be texting you an address where you will meet the executives. You are required to arrive by eight sharp. Tardiness will result in immediate disqualification."

Gotta hand it to him, he was very direct.

"Sure." I ran a hand through my tangled mess of brown hair.

"Goodbye," he said and hung up. I looked down at my cell phone. It was already almost three. I dragged my ass out of bed and took a quick shower. If I was going to be meeting people from the company, then I needed to look somewhat presentable. Leggings and an oversized black T-shirt weren't going to cut it today. I didn't have slacks, but I did have a pair of jeans without holes and a nice-looking shawl to go over a spaghetti-strap workout shirt. Shawls were my cheat to make my laundry-day shirt look nicer. My room in the apartment was a glorified closet. Walk-in, could fit a twin-size bed and a box for a nightstand. Definitely modest, but I could handle it. So could Mint.

When I left my room, Jazz[14] was in the living room at their desk. Jazz was a freelance graphic designer. They'd been doing this since before they graduated college, so they had enough clients to keep themselves paid. Normally, they'd be focused on the screen, working away, but their chair was turned to face my door. They looked at me with a blank expression and motioned for me to sit down. Well, shit.

I hadn't paid rent in three months. I kind of had. Sort of. I tossed them twenty bucks on occasion when I could. But I

---

[14] Jazz (they/them)

knew the number. I owed my roommates a lot. Like around two grand.

I could tell they were stressed, because normally they had on full makeup and a fashion-savvy outfit. Today was sweats and an oversized T-shirt they could have taken from my closet with how little they cared about their appearance. "Rent is due in four days," they said, their tone even as they eyed me carefully. I knew this was serious, and it looked like Jazz was nervous about this conversation too.

"Yep," I said with a forced smile.

"You have to pay this month."

"I will, most definitely," I nodded enthusiastically to try to ease some of the tension. They shook their head.

"I understand you're not on the lease, but we really need you to pay your share. If not, we'll rent the room to someone else."

"So, you're going to evict me?" I asked. Their eyebrows scrunched together, and they looked away. Damn. I wanted to be angry, but my brain wouldn't let me get that far. Cold sweat covered my body as I ran numbers in my head. I had to come up with seven hundred. In other words, I had to find this cat. I nodded absently.

We all had our reasons for living together. Mine was that I couldn't go back home. My mom threw me out when I said I wanted to go into preternatural studies. She thought necromancy was a phase. Right. A phase I'd had since I was eight. As far as I knew, almost no one started necromancy that early. But I filled the conditions, not that researchers fully understood how the ability to become a necromancer manifested.

Jazz had to leave home because their family wasn't cool with them doing drag. Not going by Nathan anymore was also a big deal. For Amy,[15] she just wanted to stay with friends while she did nursing school. It was more comfortable than the dorms. We'd been roomies for two years, but when the pet jobs slowed down, I couldn't afford much anymore.

"Did you hear me? You can't just blow this off like everything else in your life." Their words caught me off guard. "At some point, you have to grow up and react to stuff like this. I thought you were cool back in high school, but now your callousness is screwing with my life too. Don't you realize that we're all struggling right now? We need you to get your ass in gear for once and treat this seriously."

"Isn't being calm during a crisis a good thing?"

"There's being calm, and there's being apathetic."

"Do you think I don't care about you and Amy?" My voice was rising. This wasn't coming out of nowhere. We'd been heading this way for a long time. But I really thought Jazz knew I cared about them. I didn't want to be a bum. Life just hadn't worked out for me lately.

"I think you don't know what you're doing, and you're hoping if you drift along like you have been, things will magically work out," Jazz spat. "You could have taken a second job. When your work slowed down, you just sat on your ass. You claim you're studying, but you're not in school. Studying isn't doing you any good at this point. There's no promotion, no bonuses. Great, you'll get better

---

[15] Amy (she/her)

at bringing back gerbils. At one point, you gave a shit about getting your master's. Where is that person now?"

I sucked in air. There was no response for that one. I tried not to cry as Jazz turned back to their computer. Unlike me, my roommates were doing things with their lives. Both of them knew the path forward. I didn't even know how I'd finish my degree at this point.

So maybe Jazz was right. I could have applied for scholarships. I could have taken a class or two while working at Whataburger. It just felt like it proved my mom right if I gave in and did something else. But maybe I was just scared. And now I was dead broke and about to be evicted. I squeezed my phone in my hand and then remembered.

"I might be getting a promotion. I have to interview for it today, but I'll let you know how it goes," I said. Jazz turned from their desk and gave me a solemn nod.

"I wish you all the luck. This might be you finally moving toward something." The sincerity in their voice was enough to ease some of the tension. I had been a shitty roommate, sure, but we were still friends. That much gave me the strength to walk to my car. It didn't seem like I could ask Jazz for some snacks. I didn't want to ask either of them for anything at this point. Rent money. I just needed to pay them. I could figure out how to eat later.

When I left the apartment I saw a note taped to the door with my name on it. I snatched it, just waiting for my day to get worse. Sure enough, it said:

Forget the cat or lose your life. Your choice.

I crumpled the paper in my hand and tossed it in the waste bin. I didn't have time for this. My rent needed to get paid, and I had a test to take that I totally wasn't prepared for. Pranks were just another thing at this point. The fact that the gardener mentioned some zealot vampire made me doubt the cat had anything to do with the murders, so whoever thought this would intimidate me, clearly knew nothing about the case and definitely didn't know my desperation to get rent money. Besides, the idea of anyone trying to kill me was laughable. It didn't occur to me that no one should know about my involvement with Aphrodite outside of the police, Mrs. Bennett, and her people.

Coffee was going to be my sustenance for a hot minute, so a cafe with unlimited refills was my plan for the day. It was just until I could get a decent gig or two to help cover rent and food. Or maybe until I found this stupid cat.

Iced coffee with whole milk was my lunch and dinner. The anxiety was a lot. It felt like another being crawling under my skin. The amount of caffeine wasn't helping. I couldn't remember how many cups I had had, but it was more than five. There was no way I'd be able to Google my way through the test, so I used my phone to watch necromancy YouTube videos, bumming off the cafe's Wi-Fi. The Necromancer Daily channel was a godsend for me. The graveyard was only thirty minutes away, which meant I was able to spend hours watching videos. Hopefully, something about necromancy law or lore would come up in their tests. Anything practical and I was screwed.

By the time I needed to go to the graveyard, I was jittery and shaking. My shitty car managed to make it, despite its groaning. I was parked crooked as hell though because of the steering. It was a good thing no one else was there. I could pretend like the car wasn't mine.

After about ten minutes, a truck drove into the parking lot. On the side were the words "Undead, Inc." Maybe if I became good enough, I'd get a company car as well. Then I wouldn't have to learn how to do vehicle necromancy, not that that was a thing.

Three individuals got out of the truck. Trucks were good for the necromancers who had to raise a handful of people at a time. That's when chickens were no longer helpful and, instead, something bigger had to be sacrificed, like a cow. What did the company do with all the animal meat? Was there a designated pick-up crew or did someone tag along to grab the animal? For large animals, I wasn't sure. I unwillingly smiled remembering how Detective Malik claimed he was taking the chicken to feed his squad.

As the three people walked closer, I forced myself to stand straighter and try to be confident. An old guy who looked like Alfred[16] from Batman, an obvious Karen,[17] and a small Korean woman[18] with a vase held tightly to her chest made their way over to me. I forced a wave and a smile.

"Lily Clarke, you've caused quite a ruckus for the company," Karen said with such disdain I flinched. I knew they wouldn't like that the cops wanted an intern, but this seemed a little darker. Like they were looking for an excuse to fire me. Or at least she was.

"My name is Joseph, and I'm one of the board members for Undead, Inc. We will be testing your skills today to make

---

[16] Joseph (he/him)
[17] Karen (she/her)
[18] Chae-Won (she/her)

sure you are capable enough to handle the job you were requested for," Joseph (previously thought to be Alfred) said curtly and motioned for me to follow him. The graveyard was large with many small hills to climb over. The gravestones looked faded, like they'd been here a century too long.

Joseph stood by a grave and pointed at the recently disturbed earth. I thought he was going to ask me about tainted ground, but instead, he showed me the gravestone. "I would like you to tell me the age of the corpse. The stone is illegible. I wish you luck," he said as though this was a simple task. I'd never tried to feel out the age of someone dead before. There was a first time for everything. I'd read that necromancers could sometimes tell more about the dead by touching the earth where they were buried.

Was it too late to call it quits? This wasn't on the Necromancer Daily YouTube channel. And it seemed like the kind of thing a master's degree taught you. Jazz's face flashed in my mind. Shit. I needed to at least try. This promotion would help me be a better friend, roommate, and maybe even necromancer.

I sat down on the ground and ran my fingers over the dirt. Ever since I was a kid, I loved graveyards. It felt like a safe place, surrounded by magic.

"Anytime now," Karen called out to me. My smile faded. Right. I was here to prove myself. And hopefully, make more money.

I closed my eyes and reached out with my power. This was my first time trying anything like this. Normally, I just went with the flow. It always seemed to work out. But this time, there was pressure. My whole life could change if I just managed to do what no one had ever taught me to do before. I reached down through the earth with the coldness of my power. Necromancy always felt like a doctor's hands, cold and methodical. My power reached down deeper and deeper, until I finally felt something dead. She was small, like a child. Unlike Ricky from yesterday, she didn't belong in the dirt. She had a sense of life to her, the kind that only blood could give. "A vampire," I murmured and tried again to feel her age. No one under 18 could be changed according to the newly established Bloodletting law. It also said that you couldn't be bitten until you were of legal age as well. She was awake and waiting. I wanted to ask her for the answer, but even doing this much made my hands shake. How was I doing this? Could I ask her? Was it possible to communicate through my power? Gods, that was a terrifying thought. As I felt her eyes on me through the earth, I had a sudden thought. "She's maybe three hundred, but she was turned when she was twelve," I said hesitantly and opened my eyes. Joseph seemed to consider me more carefully. Maybe I was right?

"Chae-Won, it's your turn," he said motioning to the shortest girl. She used her long dark hair to cover her face. It was like the girl from *The Ring* walking up to me. Unlike Joseph, I could feel she was different. We were alike. Somehow, when I focused on my ability, it felt like I unlocked something. Like maybe I became stronger? It was more a feeling than a knowing. But unlike me, I knew Chae-Won wasn't an amateur. An aura of power draped around her. She was out of my league.

"Vase, what is in it?" she asked and held it tighter in her arms. I wasn't supposed to touch it, or at least she didn't want me to. It wasn't just her body language that told me that. I could feel her fear as she watched me. Something about me was making her uncomfortable. I nodded at her, more out of silent understanding of her possession rather than the task at hand. It was probably going to be ashes. Maybe I'd need to tell the age again?

Unlike last time, I didn't have graveyard dirt to help me out. Well, damn. I stared at her helplessly and she just rolled her eyes. "Your power isn't limited to the ground. Push through the air like you did with the dirt," she whispered, her mouth barely moving, and she shot a quick glance at the others. It seemed like she was trying to hide the advice from Joseph and Karen. I held out my hands but made sure not to get too close to the vase. I could feel Chae-Won's own power meeting mine as I tried to push my abilities toward her. It was like I had a mist I was trying to direct. I felt sloppy compared to the forcefield that seemed to be coming from her. I'd never felt another necromancer's power before this. I took in a deep breath and then forced my power forward. It was intrusive, and normally I tried to be respectful of people's space, but right now, I needed to know what she was holding so desperately.

It was small and felt like a swirling ball. This definitely wasn't ashes. There was a life to it. Unlike vampires who felt lifelike from blood, this was more... human. After a few moments, I realized what it was. "A soul," I spluttered. The essence danced in the container, a content but trapped soul. I'd never heard of anyone doing this. It didn't seem like it should be possible. She backed away from me. A soul was the only thing missing from zombies. "How did you do it?" She didn't answer as she quickly moved to the other two, almost hiding behind Joseph.

"Now, it's my turn," Karen said with her *I-want-to-see-your-manager* smile. Great. Out of the three, she seemed like the one most likely to fire me. "You lack training and a degree, so I doubt you'll succeed or even know what I'm talking about." Her words came out like a disappointed sigh, but I could see her sneer. "You must make a totem. On a handful of graves are boxes with materials you can use. Some of these materials will neutralize the totem's power. If you choose any of these, then you will fail."

She seemed to think my failing was automatic. Granted, I had no idea what a totem was to begin with. I pulled out my phone and did a quick Google.

"No phones," Joseph said apologetically. I sighed. I didn't even get a chance to see the definition before he caught me.

Unlike the other two, Karen at least told me what failing meant, and it seemed like I'd find out immediately. I could have failed the other two for all I knew.

I walked to the closest box. The box had ribbon, splinters of wood, and bones. None of which seemed to be from an animal I knew. There were small skulls with sharp teeth, as well as weirdly curved tails. Finally, I noticed something that looked like a leg or arm bone, maybe four inches long. I grabbed that one.

I looked over the wood but none of them seemed right, so I moved onto the next box. There had to have been like five different boxes to look through, and I had no idea what any of the items meant or what they were even for. Great. I already failed. It'd help if I knew anything about what I was making. Was it some kind of necromancy tool? That seemed like the most likely answer.

This box was almost fully wood. I felt my fingers drawn to thick splinters of cedar and yew. I picked them up and held them with my bone. The next box had ribbon. There were frilly ones, bright ones, and ones so thick they might as well have been yarn. None of the ribbons seemed right.

I glanced around the graveyard and noticed a crypt. I couldn't look away from it as my feet moved on their own. Just like the graves, the wording on the outside was mere whispers of what had been written there before. Given its apparent age, I didn't think the words would have been English anyway. Texas was part of Mexico for a while, after all. And there were others too, such as different native groups. Who knew how long this had been here.

"Why did you pick this graveyard," I asked as I stroked the stone. The crypt was maybe eight by eight, and the stone seemed like marble. But I didn't know much about these things, so it could have been anything.

"This is the oldest graveyard we could find in the area. It's been many different things over the last several centuries, but it has always held the dead," Chae-Won said. I hadn't expected her to be the one to share, but I appreciated it. There was a crack with a piece of the stone dangling from it, almost breaking off but not quite. I grabbed the piece and clutched it so tightly in my hand that I could feel it cut into my palm. I flinched as I felt the hot liquid on my hand. Damn. Why did I do that?

I lifted my hand to check out the damage, but the piece began to move and shifted onto the wound. The blood soaked into the cluster of materials in my hand. My stomach twisted. Sure, I saw dead things on a regular but watching inanimate objects drink my blood was on a whole different level. I shook my head and looked back at the totem. Okay, this thing was creepy as fuck, but I still needed this promotion. The pieces in my hand weren't ready, not yet. They needed something to keep them together. I guessed that was the reason for the ribbons, but they didn't seem personal enough. I mean, I just fed the thing my blood.

I yanked a few strands of my hair out and used them to tie the pieces together. Before I could knot it, the totem moved on its own and fused together. A single piece. I didn't think I could take it apart even if I wanted to. All traces of my blood were gone too.

"Are you not going to add more?" Karen asked, her smile wide and sinister. She obviously didn't see the thing drink my blood and fuse. I shook my head, no longer intimidated by her. My totem had power. I could feel it. I did it right. Karen came forward to look at the totem, but Chae-Won held up a hand to stop her.

"As the only other necromancer, I should be the one to verify," she said with confidence I hadn't seen in her before. She didn't move to touch it, instead, she just examined my totem from a distance. "You have successfully completed all tests. We will be in contact with the next steps."

Karen's scowl was so deep it looked like it'd cause wrinkles, but Joseph had a small smile on his face, as though he knew it would play out like this. I flashed Karen the brightest smile I could muster.

"So how much is the pay?"

Chapter 5

According to Joseph, there would be no discussion of pay until the contract was finalized with the police. Normally, that'd be fine, but I was down to three days until rent was due. It was pretty clear that the company didn't expect me to pass the tests in the first place, so they hadn't prepared to talk pay. I wondered if there was a standard rate or if it'd change since I wasn't a college graduate. Currently, I was getting twenty an hour and fifty cents a mile, which meant gas money and groceries since I only had three cases a week. If the police paid any more than that, then maybe I'd be able to pay bills for once.

When I got home, there was no note on the door, which was nice. I had hoped my roommates would be home. I wanted to tell them about the exam and the new promotion, but it was probably better they weren't. I didn't have all the details yet anyway. My bed was calling my name.

I glanced at the totem in my hand. What was this thing anyway? I turned it around, examining it as though I didn't just put it together like an hour ago. When I woke up, I could look into this thing. Figure out what the hell a totem was.

I set the totem on the nightstand, switched into a onesie, and ignored my stomach as it growled. Maybe when I woke up, Undead, Inc., would have an answer for me that involved me being able to buy food. It was barely after midnight. Hopefully, today would be a better day.

I was in a dining hall, like one you'd see in those old castles overseas. The only lights were torches, which seemed extremely inconvenient. I was wearing a floor-length white dress and slippers, probably the most elegant thing I'd ever worn in my life. What an odd dream. The dining table had several chairs around it, but there was no food, no dining set, not even a centerpiece. I almost left the room, but then someone appeared in front of me. It was the vampire from before, Hale.

He looked just as gorgeous, but this time, he was dressed like some noble from long ago. He had on black slacks, a white long-sleeve shirt that had puffy arms but a thin wrist, and a black vest. I guess my outfit was meant to match.

"I'm not much for roleplay," I said, ignoring my dark history as a teenager on forums.

"I thought this might be a nice change of pace," he smiled, and when he did, the room became brighter.

"Are you really here? Like is this some kind of vampire magic thing?" I asked. Every ounce of preternatural knowledge I had was gone. There was a word for this. If a vampire was making this dream happen, then some kind of word existed to explain it. Thrall. That's right. "Did you thrall me?"

His expression darkened, and he was no longer looking at me. I wanted to take it back. If this was supposed to be my reprieve from all the nonsense earlier, then I should just enjoy it. There was no reason to accuse some hot vamp of getting into my mind. Besides, thralling humans was a felony, and accusing anyone of a felony seemed like a bad idea.

"I prodded your mind just enough to be able to do this. I didn't thrall you. I wasn't intending on joining your dreams either, until a complication," he said. His voice was quiet, but in the emptiness of the room, I could hear him clearly.

I knew enough from school that joining dreams and thrall weren't that far apart. Thrall was when a vampire tainted a human's mind. It was permanent. Anytime during that human's lifetime, the vampire could summon the human to them and order the human to do anything, and the human would willingly and happily do it. If he could join my dreams, then that meant I was one step under thrall. I should have been scared, but with everything else on my plate, I just didn't have the capacity to care about one extra thing. What I really wanted to know was the pay from the police.

"I don't really like dresses," I pointed out. Hale's eyes widened, and soon he was laughing, full-on snort-laughing. I laughed with him, more from the sound of his own laughter than my comment. His face was a deep red, which I thought was impossible for vampires, when he stopped himself abruptly and covered his mouth with his hand. It seemed like he was shy. At this point, he was already in my dreams. There was no reason to be shy now.

He shook his head. "I hate my laugh. I always wind up snorting." I waited for him to say something else, but when he didn't, I busted up laughing even harder than before.

"So? It's just a laugh. I'm not going to judge you for it," I said. "I *can* change out of this thing, right?"

"You can change your clothes by just imagining what you want to wear. This is a dream, after all."

I looked down at my clothes. Sure enough, they changed on their own to my pajamas.

"I guess I'll change too," Hale nodded, his face back to normal as he was suddenly in pants and a Chevelle T-shirt. "We did get sidetracked though," he admonished.

I didn't care, despite his serious tone. Whatever he could say wouldn't be any worse than pending eviction, as well as suddenly having to pretend to be a real necromancer working for real investigators.

"Yeah, yeah, yeah, what's the issue?" I asked and stuffed my hands in my pockets, because in dreams, girls could have real pockets.

"Thanks to our fateful meeting, my enemies believe we are intimate and are trying to have you eliminated." Hale sighed and brushed his blond hair back. "It's my fault. I shouldn't have touched you that much. The kiss was definitely-" he trailed off. It was just a forehead kiss, but the thought alone had me blushing again.

Wait. "Eliminated" implied killed. Did people want me dead?! The thought that someone might want me dead was so absurd that I was laughing all over again. Full, doubled-over laughing. He crossed his arms over his chest as he waited for me to finish. When I could finally breathe, he continued. "I'm not joking, Lily. This is my fault, so I will be sending a bodyguard to watch over you until I can handle the situation." I stopped breathing. So, this was real?

"What makes you so special that being near a girl would put her in danger?" I asked, unable to hide my skepticism. He was just a hot vampire. Was this some kind of kink? Was he trying to "dark romance" me into being with him?

48

Hale moved closer to me until our faces were mere inches apart.

"Vampire hierarchy is a thing, doll," he said with a teasing smile that felt misplaced. "There's your standard vampire, a vampire who has been around for a hundred years or more, and then Master Vampires." His violet eyes flashed with power, swirls of purple pulling me in. "This means I'm powerful enough to be responsible for a sizeable number of my kind. And currently, that also means I get to advocate for vampire rights in both the Texas Senate and the United States Congress."

My eyes were wide as I listened to him. This stuff wasn't talked about in community college. If I was outside of my dream, then I'd definitely be taking notes.

"But still, why would anyone care?" I managed to get out.

Hale sighed softly and took a step back. "Because there's competition for my role. People who are desperate to find a weakness outside of a snort while laughing." He looked so tired in that moment, and I wanted to reach out. I almost did. But then he turned back to me. "That's why I'm giving you a bodyguard. My best."

I didn't believe him until he said bodyguard. That shouldn't have made a difference, but the thought of someone appearing in my life to try to prevent my death... it was just so weird. Like, everything he said just sounded like nonsense.

"My car itself is a death trap, and I choke on a regular. What do you mean 'eliminated'?!" I asked. My voice sounded foreign. If I could choke on ice tomorrow and die, what's the point of someone going out of their way to cause it? Why would anyone care about me, especially in relation to some guy way out of my league?

"I believe they're trying to hurt me by causing your death," he explained. He wasn't looking at me anymore. I could feel his guilt. It was a chance encounter. And now, here he was feeling responsible for the life of some girl.

"But it wouldn't hurt you if I died," I retorted and wished I hadn't. He flinched, and his eyes had the kind of vampire romance melancholy you have to pay money to see.

"I'd be responsible. So, yes, it would hurt me." The anger in his voice took me by surprise. I wanted to question him, but then his eyes were on me again and I stopped. His expression was cold and almost cruel, but there was a sadness to it. How did I know he was sad? "Once you're safe, you will never hear from me again."

With that, I woke up. My cat was kneading my hip and purring as though she knew I needed a massage after the dream I had. I scratched Mint behind the ears and slowly made my way back to reality. I blinked at the memory of Hale in my dream. He said I was being threatened. My thoughts wandered to the threat on my door earlier. That was about a cat though and was definitely a prank. But still. Kind of ironic that someone threatened my life the same day I was told people wanted to kill me for a completely different reason.

I had crashed so early that it was only ten in the morning. This meant I had an actual day to find Mrs. Bennett's cat. The thought alone made me groan. It wasn't until I was stumbling to the living room that I realized Hale had been serious about a bodyguard, because on the couch was a man[19] I'd never seen before. He was Japanese and looked to be in his early thirties. His eyes were brown and his hair stark black. Although his face's features were soft, his expression was anything but. After all, his all-black attire and mannerisms screamed "bodyguard." And yet, he was gorgeous as hell. Where Hale was blond with violet eyes and the soft strength of a prince, Rin was darker, harder, and seemed like a knight. But maybe I'd been reading too many romance novels.

Jazz had their headphones on and was working away on their desktop. I had a feeling they were the one who let this guy in.

"I was going to head out. Does that mean you're coming too?" I asked, not really sure how this worked. Jazz's eyes narrowed.

"You're leaving in that?" They asked, making me look down and flush. Onesie pajamas, right. Probably should change out of those. I rushed back to my room and forced myself to wake up. I was suddenly being judged and looked after by a very muscular and potentially deadly stranger. I gave my teeth a quick brush and forced a comb through my bedhead. The totem was on my bed now. I didn't remember moving it. I grabbed it and shoved the thing in my pocket.

Wait a second! He worked for some uber-hot vampire. Maybe he'd be good at finding missing cats? Like, have an information network and stuff that can help?

---

[19] Rin (he/him)

Suddenly the thought of having some dangerous guy tail me didn't seem half bad. I grinned to myself and stepped out into the living room.

"Can you possibly look into people named Sebastian in the area? He kidnapped a cat that I need to find before Friday," I explained and pulled out my phone. "The cat looks like this. If you could do this for me, it would mean a great deal. Please?" The silence made me want to retract everything I just said. He did not look like he wanted anything to do with me, let alone offer to help me out.

"You need help finding a cat? I could have my followers keep an eye out for her. Just shoot me the pics," Jazz said. I didn't think they were paying attention, but apparently, they were. That's when I noticed their headphones weren't plugged into anything. So, they were secretly listening this whole time, little snoop. I smiled and forwarded the pics. Jazz had a pretty big following online. They did makeup tutorials and drag show reactions, so they had several million followers on YouTube and about a million on Twitch. If anyone could use their influence to find Aphrodite, it'd be them.

"Is this what you're going to be doing for the foreseeable future? And with this little amount of information?" the bodyguard questioned, his voice low but not as gruff as I expected it to be.

"Yes," I said. Despite my insecurities and reservations, I needed to get this done. I glanced over at Jazz. I didn't want to let my friends down anymore.

"Text the info to this number. I can't be bothered to watch you run in circles for Gods know how long," he sighed and showed me a number on his phone. I did as he asked and smiled to myself.

"Okay cool, thank you so much," I said, then froze. "I never introduced myself, did I?"

"No, and I didn't either," he smirked as though my sudden realization amused the crap out of him.

"Lily Clarke," I said with a sigh.

"Rin." No last name. I knew better than to ask though.

"Wanna join me for breakfast, Rin?" I asked and grabbed my keys. He shrugged his shoulders and stood up. The walk to my car was quiet; however, once he saw what I was driving, he immediately took my keys from me.

"No," is all he said as he led me to a black BMW with temporary plates. I pressed my lips together but didn't say anything. That is, until I saw the heated seats. It didn't matter that it was 90-plus outside, heated seats were going on to the max! I gave him the address to the nearest coffee shop with the full intention of having another iced coffee day. Friday was only a couple of days away. Once I had been paid, I could treat myself!

When I ordered my iced coffee and sat down, once again, Rin said "No." Food. This man, whom I had never seen before in my life, bought me food. My heart fluttered as I looked at the blueberry muffin. This man was a saint.

"You work for Hale, right?" I asked as I took a big bite. The look of disgust on this man's face nearly choked me. I told Hale I'd die from choking before an assassin got me, but I didn't realize I'd have the chance to demonstrate it.

"You got in the car with a man you'd never met before and accepted food from him," he said the words slowly. This felt an awful lot like a van with some candy. I could already see the regret on his face.

"But now you're here to make sure I don't do dumb stuff like this," I said in the hope I'd reassure him.

"I think in Texas they say 'bless your heart' in these situations," he deadpanned. Well then, it looked like I was going to have fun with this one. Rin was definitely feisty.

"So, is feeding me part of your gig?" I continued as I stuffed the muffin in my face. Rin tilted his head and looked at me as though I was some specimen he just came across.

"Hale gave me his credit card," Rin said as a waitress came up with a sandwich for him. It looked like tuna. Apparently having a credit card meant food. Works for me.

I felt the totem in my pocket and paused. I pulled it out and looked at the strange thing. It hummed in my hand and radiated a certain coldness.

For just a moment, I forgot about my hunger and just stared at the totem. I pulled out my phone and checked the Necromancer Daily YouTube channel. I searched through their videos trying to find anything on totems, but no. Just how to tell if you raised a possum or if it's playing dead and some basic videos on raising the dead and undead types. Nothing overtly useful currently, although I saved the possum video for later.

I googled necromancer totems to see what would pop up, and to my surprise, I found out Undead, Inc., really was trying to sabotage me. It's rare for any necromancer to be able to create a totem. It requires a high ability level and only an eighth of the necromancers currently known are able to use one. I guess the company thought that an intern wouldn't be able to make one.

And yet, despite Google providing me the insight, it failed to mention what the fuckeroni a totem actually was. I scowled and kept scrolling through search results.

My phone rang, and I almost dropped it. Undead, Inc., was calling! They probably had my answer by now. I could barely contain my excitement. I was powerful enough to have a totem after all; of course they'd be paying me more.

"Do I gotta stay near you or can I," I trailed off as he glared. Okay, right. I do the thing, and he does his thing, and we'll be doing our things together. I stepped outside with Rin close behind and answered the phone.

"Good afternoon, I'm calling to give you verbal confirmation that you have passed all the qualifiers to work with the Preternatural Department of North Texas," the voice said. I already knew this from last night.

"Thank you."

"You will receive an email shortly with updated information on your pay with our company as well as the commission you will receive from the police department. Negotiations will be handled by the company. Payment will be received after the completion of an assignment, as usual," he said and waited. I gave a sound of agreement, although at this point, I just wanted the email. "Congratulations, Miss Clarke, on your promotion." He sounded anything but pleased as he hung up the phone.

"That was brief," Rin said from beside me. I didn't have a retort. Instead, I looked down at my phone. I should probably keep looking into totems, but my hands were trembling. I'd be getting an email. This email would most likely change my life.

I noticed my half-eaten muffin and was quickly pulled from my thoughts. Right. Distractions. Definitely needed right now. I finished my food without tasting it as Rin continued to stare at me as though trying to solve a puzzle. He didn't seem annoyed anymore, which was great, but he was definitely not thrilled either.

It took about fifteen minutes before my notifications went off. An email!

The email was more than I'd hoped for. I was getting paid real money now. No raise with Undead, Inc., but working with the police was decent money. Two hundred dollars per victim raised. Yeah, people were supposedly trying to kill me. But right now, I just got told I might be able to consistently pay rent every month for forever after this. Life didn't seem that bad.

Chapter 6

Rin had gotten the information on Sebastian much quicker than I expected. The groomer had security cameras, which Patty conveniently forgot to mention. I don't know how he convinced her to let him see them. I had a feeling he probably did something illegal to get the info, but I wasn't going to say anything. From there, Rin was able to ID the guy and find his place of work. Sebastian was a stripper. He also had a rap sheet that was covered in violent offenses. There ain't no rest for the wicked.

"Aren't you going to tell me I shouldn't be doing this?" I asked Rin as we waited in line outside the male strip club. He had his hands by his side and looked casual, but I could see the way he was scanning the crowd. If something happened, he'd protect me.

"Would it matter if I did?" he asked. I pressed against the brick wall and sighed. Yeah, probably not. Even so, I wanted someone to try to tell me not to. Maybe point out I was being a dumbass and shouldn't confront a potential kidnapper. All of that sounded reasonable, like something someone who cared about me would say. Jazz and Amy would have if I had told them about it, but I didn't want them involved. It was time to act like an adult for once. Which apparently meant getting into dangerous situations to pay rent.

When we entered, I was hit with the smell of sweat and desperation. Women were screaming at the stage, which was the most lit-up part of the club. Standing about five feet above the main floor, men were thrusting their hips for the audience with just thongs and cowboy hats on. I looked away quickly and tried to remember how to breathe through the fumes. Yes. Strippers. Naked men. It's a thing.

I should have remembered that's what strip clubs were for. Men without clothes. Damn.

It's not like I was a virgin, but nudity was usually a pretty intimate thing for me. Here though, the girls were throwing money at these guys and catcalling. There was no romance, but there were plenty of suggestive smiles and flexing. I picked a table in the corner that had leftover drinks and a stickiness I didn't want to identify. It was loud, but the waiters were attentive. Within seconds, a girl[20] came by with two glasses of water for us. I'd never been to one of these places before, but I knew better than to think water was given out freely.

She had on a black vest over a white blouse and wore black trousers. It looked way too hot to be wearing that in a place like this. Her eyes were the color of a raging ocean and looked over at us like we were insignificant. Her long blond hair was pulled back in a tight ponytail. Rather than leave to go to the next table, she waited as though expecting something. Rin pulled out a twenty and slipped it to her. "We're looking for a guy named Sebastian," he said. She nodded, her face a mask of indifference, and left us alone.

I shrunk into the table and tried to ignore the guys in thongs who were walking around with ones in their G-strings. Even so, Rin was the hottest one here. "Is it too late to go?" I grumbled as a particularly loud group of women were begging for a lap dance. One of them had just gotten a divorce, and this was her divorce party. I only knew that because of the balloons that said *Free at Last, Hoes over Bros, We Never Liked Him Anyway, Ring Returned to Sender*, and *His Dick Was Small*.

---

[20] Ariel (she/they/he)

"You're the one who wanted to be here," Rin pointed out. He had a smug smile on his face as he looked at me. I frowned and covered my face with my hands as another guy walked by with his dick almost hanging out.

The girls started to scream, and I peeked over to see that a guy was over there, grinding into one of the girls as she was sitting in her chair. I noticed a table near me with barstools for chairs instead of ones with backs and grabbed one. Now there was no way for someone to think I wanted a lap dance.

"I had no idea it was going to be this much," I stumbled out. Rin shook his head at me, but it wasn't in a mean way. Instead, it was more like having an older brother. My actual brother was younger than me by about ten years, so I never got to experience the whole "older sibling teasing me" thing.

"You went to a strip club and weren't expecting to see skin."

His deadpan made me groan. Okay, yeah, I was being silly. I got that now. But he didn't have to be a dick about it. Rin handed me a stack of ones. It was hefty, like maybe fifty total. How many ramen packets was this? Maybe a hundred if they were on that fifty-cent sale? But then there's tax. Rin looked at me, making me realize I had been staring at the cash for way too long.

"What's this for?" I asked as a stripper came up to us. He had the standard cowboy hat, but also a pet collar, leash, leather suspenders, and a harness with a lock around his crotch. Several sweaty dollar bills were sticking out of it. I guess I knew what the ones were for now.

"Who wants to be my master?" He asked with a sly smile. His body smelled thick with arousal and makeup, I leaned back as far away from him as I could, but that only drew his attention to the wad of cash on the table, which made his smile widen. "How about we get a private room?" he continued and held out the leash.

I shook my head as words abandoned me. Somehow the leash made its way into my hands. "We're looking for someone named Sebastian," I stuttered. The stripper blew me a kiss and tugged the leash to gently lead me.

"My name is Angel, and I'll be your entertainer this evening," he winked. I would have blown it off thinking this was a different guy, but I saw the way his eyes narrowed momentarily when I said I was looking for Sebastian, which made me snap back to reality. The catnapper!

We entered a room with a red velvet curtain for a door. As soon as the curtain closed, I dropped the leash and pulled out my phone. "I've still got money for you, but I need some answers rather than... whatever it is you do," I said with an attempt at sounding like I knew what I was doing. I absolutely did not.

Rin adjusted so he was standing halfway between me and Sebastian. The stripper was still smiling at us, but something had gone dark in his face. Like he was ready to hurt us if he needed to.

"How could I say no to such a pretty girl?" he asked with over-the-top chivalry. I cringed. Yeah, I knew I wasn't pretty, but to have him fake it so strongly hurt.

"Do you recognize this cat?"

I could feel his energy shift. Rather than wanting to run, he preferred to fight. The aggression was hidden behind his smile, but I could still feel it. I couldn't explain how, but I knew. He wanted to hurt me.

"Nah, should I?"

"It's funny you say you don't recognize the cat when we have you on video carrying her out of a pet lounge on Tuesday," Rin said. I wasn't expecting him to jump in. It was comforting though, feeling the aggression shift from me to someone else. At least he'd be able to handle it. I assumed the bodyguard job meant he had experience with this kind of thing.

"Are you sure it was me?" he asked and undid the collar at his throat. I didn't notice it before, but he had a whip attached to his hip, which he pulled out and began to play with. He went from asking for a master to behaving like someone who could dominate. I shivered.

"Yes."

"We're at a bit of a standstill, aren't we?"

Rin glanced at me. My body was so cold, and I knew I was shaking. I'd never confronted someone before, especially not like this. I just wanted this to be nicer, easier. Maybe he could hand me the cat, and I'd be on my way. Why couldn't he work with me?

"Doll, I gotta confess. I did kidnap the cat. I was ordered to by a guy. Didn't know him, and he paid upfront. So, I picked her up and was supposed to kill her. I couldn't do it with my hands like that, so I tossed the little thing over a bridge off 183."

The drastic change in his attitude threw me, but whatever made him do it, I was grateful. Rin's eyes narrowed as he stared the stripper down.

"We got what we came for, let's go," I said and reached for his arm. Yeah, it sucked the cat was dead, but at least I had some kind of an answer finally. Plus, I could leave the strip club, which was something I wanted to do from the moment I entered.

"Do you realize how long of a road that is?" Rin scoffed.

"Oh." Right, we're in Texas. "Where exactly-" I started but then stopped. Sebastian's expression had changed. The softness was gone. Instead, his face was contorted into pure rage.

"What did you do to me?" he asked so softly I almost didn't hear him. I instinctively took a step back. His anger. It was suffocating. "I would never have told you that shit." It felt like needles were pricking into my skin dragging me under into a heat that burned so strong I felt faint. Was this his rage?

I opened my mouth to respond. But I didn't know. He just got nicer. I thought he wanted us to leave so he got talkative. No. That was a lie. I knew it was weird. I just didn't want to think about it. It was too much. Like maybe I controlled him. And now that I could feel his anger, I knew that I did. I had controlled him into being helpful and kind. And now he wanted to destroy me for it.

"Back off," Rin said. He wasn't angry, but I knew he was ready to fight if needed. Sebastian's eyes never left me. With all the rage on his face, he looked like the kind of man who could throw a cat off a bridge.

"What the fuck did you do to me?!"

I flinched. What was I supposed to say?

He didn't give me time to think any more as he lunged for me. He flicked his whip. It barely missed my face. I fell to the floor. My heart pounded as Rin knocked the whip out of his hand.

I screamed. Rin pinned him to the ground. "Are you done?" Rin asked.

"Is she done screwing with my head?!"

I hid behind one of the couches and tried to focus on my breathing. He wanted me dead. Hale said people wanted me dead, but this was different. I'd never seen someone hate me this much. Prick, prick, prick. The sensation covered me, needles digging into skin until it felt like I'd bleed out from the pain, but there were no visible marks.

Suddenly there was a bang, and Sebastian was in front of my face. I screamed and held out my hands. All his anger. I wanted it to be sent back to him. I couldn't take it, and he was the one feeling it. So, shouldn't he have it back? He stopped mid-reach, and his eyes widened.

"What?" he asked, his voice quiet.

That's when cuts began to appear all over his body. Blood dripped down. It was like a physical manifestation of what I had been feeling. After a few seconds, I couldn't make out his features anymore. He was just a puddle of blood. The anger was gone now. Instead, he was full of fear. He opened his mouth and choked on the blood that slipped in.

I covered my mouth with my hands as tears streamed down my face. What did I do?!

The waitress from earlier walked in just as Sebastian collapsed. She didn't seem surprised and instead held the curtain open wider. Rin grabbed my arm and dragged me out. "But-" I started. She held up her hand to silence me.

"A priest will handle it. Go," she said, her tone neutral but firm. I could feel that he was alive, but how could I possibly know that?! My eyes were blurred from all the tears, but Rin managed to help me miss most of the tables and chairs on our way out. Sure enough, at the door, a priest[21] in all white walked in. I thought it was a stripper outfit until he looked at me and smiled. There was nothing seductive about it.

"No need for tears, you'll be okay," he said a little too knowingly as Rin led me out into the darkness. The priest managed to slip a card into my hand. I looked down, and it said *Priest Christopher from the Dallas branch of the Church of Light*.

Rin didn't say a word to me the entire way. It wasn't until we got in the car that he turned to me.

"Don't you ever do something that dangerous again," he said so seriously I struggled to breathe.

"I don't know what the fuck I did, so how can I stop doing it?" I spluttered, making Rin stop to look at me.

"You don't know what you did?"

I shook my head quickly.

All the friendliness from before was gone. I could feel it though. He was angry, sure, but he was also scared. I scared him. I nodded slowly, and he sighed. "I don't even

---

[21] Priest Christopher (he/him)

know what to call what you did back there. Are you a psychic or something?"

A psychic? No. There was no way. Schools test for that once you get to college. I was just a necromancer. I gripped the church card in my hand. Looks like I might be something else too.

Chapter 7

I got a call from the police department, which was great for getting rid of the silence. Rin still wasn't talking to me. My phone was connected to the Bluetooth, so Rin could hear the call too. I figured there was some kind of confidentiality issue with that, but I didn't have much choice.

"My name is Parker Adams.[22] Is this Lily Clarke?" He sounded young, too young to work for the police.

"Yeah, it's me," I said.

"Ms. Clarke, there's another body. You need to go to the morgue in Fort Worth. I'll send you the address by text. This is an ongoing investigation, so we are requiring absolute silence about the details of the case. You are an outside consultant, but only an observer. No pictures and no phones inside the morgue. Time is crucial. What's your ETA?"

I pulled out my phone and showed the address to Rin. He clicked a couple buttons and the GPS showed on the display in the car. This was super fancy.

"About thirty minutes."

Parker sighed. "Fine. Try to get here faster. No one goes home until you get finished."

Well, jeez. Way to make me feel welcome. My hands were shaking. I had to do it again. Somehow, I had to raise another human. Could I even do it a second time?

He hung up before I could say anything else. It was just as well. I didn't know if I could say anything anyway. All that

---

[22] Parker Adams (he/him)

blood earlier... and here I was about to spill some again. At least this time it wouldn't be human.

"Why are the police asking some kid to go to a morgue?" I wasn't expecting Rin to ask, but I guess since he was giving me a ride, I should tell him. I was totally a walking liability with the police.

"I'm a necromancer. I raise the dead," I said, but I couldn't keep my voice from breaking. The email said I would get paid $200 per dead body raised. Even though I was nervous, this didn't seem nearly as terrifying as what I did to Sebastian earlier. Was he alive? He was when I left, but...

When we arrived, Rin wasn't allowed inside. I expected as much. Rin did not look pleased. I flashed him an apologetic smile as I was given a police escort through the plain white building. The air had a dry chill to it. It was foreboding. The two policemen escorts looked like those asshole jocks I used to see at the bar by my old college. They were buff in a way that was made to intimidate. You can always tell the people who work out for strength or appearance. These guys wanted the look.

The room they led me to was at the end of the hall, and there were already plenty of people inside. Detective Malik, a deputy, and a woman[23] I'd never seen before. She was tall even without her black heels and had on a pencil skirt and a tailored V-neck. Her brown hair was pulled into a bun, and her eyes were narrowed as she looked me over.

---

[23] Jennifer Caldwell (she/her)

"You took over thirty minutes to arrive," she said with a tut.

"She arrived sooner than I expected," Malik countered. He scowled at her. They must have had some words before I showed up. Cool. I wasn't the only person that instantly hated her.

"My name is Jennifer Caldwell, and I am one of the top necromancers at Undead, Inc. I am here to ensure you can complete the tasks required by you during the probationary period," she said. No one had warned me, but maybe that was the point. "Tardiness is not a good impression." Her face wasn't a good impression either.

"Okay, so… how long will you be stalking me?" I asked and moved closer to the dead body. The carcass seemed way friendlier than this chick. I probably should have been nicer since she was above me at the company. Given the day I had had, I didn't feel all that nice, especially since she couldn't shush her face.

"Until I decide you're ready." Her smile was so sharp, I winced. Another person to constantly judge me.

"However, you'll be the one to do the raising." This came from the detective. He motioned toward the victim,[24] and I grimaced. Another man, but this one was younger. He seemed like a high schooler or maybe a freshman in college. His closed eyes and pale features made him look asleep, but the innards ripped out of his stomach said otherwise. Gods, it smelled like a mixture of sweetbreads and fermented beans. So gross.

"You got a chicken?" I asked. The deputy quickly ran to the back of the room and grabbed a crate with not one, not

---

[24] Marcas James (he/him)

two, but three chickens in it. I mean, if I couldn't figure it out the first try, then at least I had a couple more attempts ready to go. Somehow, I doubted Jennifer would let me try again.

"You have a totem, and you're still going to use an animal?" Jennifer asked condescendingly. I had no idea what that meant, so I just ignored her.

The deputy had an apologetic smile on his face. He was short, with freckles, brown eyes, chubby cheeks, and a rapidly receding hairline. He couldn't be older than thirty. I knelt by the crate.

After the last chicken, I'd googled a bit more about how to do this. This time, I wouldn't drop the chicken. Especially in front of Jennifer. The deputy didn't offer me any help as I pulled one out of the crate. I didn't expect him to. He was looking at me as though he didn't think I belonged here. Everyone was in uniform except me and Jennifer. At least she was dressed up. I just had my bloody leggings and shirt. It's kind of funny that no one was asking me about it. Then again, I was about to bleed a chicken. I guess they figured I had just reanimated something else. Better than suspecting me of attempted murder. Chills ran down my spine as I remembered the way Sebastian bled. I forced myself to take a deep breath. I had a job to do.

I paused and looked back at the table with the dead guy. I'd never raised something away from dirt before. Would it be much different or much of the same? The pets I'd done had all been in graveyards. This seemed a bit high level. I dumped the chicken back in the crate and pulled out my phone.

70

"No cell phones," the deputy said with a nervous smile, as though he didn't want to tell me this but was just doing his job. Right. I'd forgotten. Using my phone could be seen as potentially sharing intimate info from a crime scene, like pictures or recordings. Ugh. Couldn't I just tell them I was inept and needed to make sure I could figure out how to do my job? I had never thought to look up whether I could raise the dead in a morgue before. The googling barely popped up anything before I was stuck putting my phone up.

I smiled sheepishly at everyone and tried to keep my cool. I was the center of attention. Great. The chicken seemed much more wary of me and tried to peck at my hands. I had to reach with my left hand like I was going to grab it, then sneak attack when it pecked again. I barely managed to get it by the neck. Ew, I was going to have to break it like I did last time. But at least I knew it would still move after. I held the bird tightly with one hand and the body with the other. At some point, I was going to have to figure out a humane way to do this.

Once it stopped squirming, I pulled my pocketknife out. A few splatters of blood and I'd hopefully have my zombie. The blood soaked into the body, and I set the chicken down on the floor, away from the crate. I didn't want his buddies to see his corpse.

When I saw the blood, a part of me froze and thought about Sebastian. He was *covered* in blood. But a priest showed up. Priests can heal wounds. Sebastian was alive. He had to be. Gods, I needed him to be alive.

"Does my team get fried chicken again?" Malik asked with a smirk. I jumped in surprise, my thoughts forced back to the present. I shoved my emotions down and instead paid attention to what was happening in front of me.

"No way," his deputy said, his eyes wide. "You got the chicken from her zombie raising?!" His disbelief was enough to make me relax. It felt like this was Malik's way of encouraging me. There's no way he knew what I'd been through. Even so, apparently I just needed some morbid humor, and I could raise a guy from the dead.

My totem thrummed in my pocket, so I took it out and held it in my fingers while I let the cold power within me release and cling to the body. The zombie's stomach sewed itself back together. It wasn't until the smell of rot went away that I noticed his eyes were open and staring at me. He had the scent of a sweaty boy, which was way better than spilled guts. The adrenaline and exhaustion from last time weren't here. I looked down at the totem in confusion. Was this the totem's doing? I really needed to figure out what the heck this thing actually was.

The deputy gasped, his hands over his mouth as he looked at my zombie.

"Hello, good sir," I grinned and reached out my hand to help him sit up. It was a ridiculous offer given the fact that he was tall as hell, buff, and seemed way more flexible than me. At the same time, he was also recently raised in a room full of strangers. He nodded curtly at me as he took in his surroundings. He had dark brown hair that curled around his ears. His eyes were brilliant blue, and he had a small scar above the right side of his mouth. I forced myself to stop checking out a dead guy and motioned toward Detective Malik.

"I'm going to need you to answer this nice man's questions."

The "nice man" stepped forward with zero emotion on his face. His deputy was standing at attention beside him but couldn't hide his awe at the zombie. He wasn't at the graveyard with us the other day, so I guess zombie raisings weren't standard issue in police investigations. It made sense since the cost was so high. Not every crime got the same amount of funds to solve it.

"Can you confirm your name for me?" the detective asked.

"What's your name?" the zombie asked me. He was blatantly ignoring the detective. I tensed. Did I do something wrong? Zombies weren't supposed to ask me questions like this. Jennifer was furiously writing notes in a journal. Yeah, this was definitely a sign of a fuck up.

"I'm Lily. But I don't want you to talk to me. The detective has questions for you. Can you please focus on him?"

Malik raised an eyebrow at me. It was probably because I said "please." Why shouldn't I be polite to a guy I reanimated?

"Marcas James," he said, but his eyes were on me. There was a connection between us. I could feel it. He needed me at that moment and was expecting something. But I didn't know what to do, so I stayed quiet.

The detective pulled out a photo. "Do you know this vampire[25]?" he asked. I couldn't help being nosy. I looked at it too. The photo was of a girl that looked to be around his same age. She had a giant smile and a book in her hands in the photo. I thought it was a girlfriend at first with

[25] Camilla (she/her)

the way he stared at her. But then I noticed the second body. A table over was an outline of a body with a white sheet over it, but the head was detached and to the side. I shivered. What kind of beast could decapitate a vampire? They were way stronger than humans. It'd have to be a were-animal or another vampire. It was the only thing that made sense.

"Yeah, this is Camilla. She works at the warehouse with me," he said using the present tense. Maybe he didn't know he was dead either. Guilt tugged at my stomach, but I couldn't say anything. If he realized it now, then he might wig out and be unhelpful. I knew from experience with animals that you needed to keep the zombies as calm and content as possible or they'd break. It was always heartbreaking when a dog realized they couldn't go home with their owners. Humans realizing they were dead was no different

I thought about the guy from the other day. The gardener. He wanted to stay alive just a bit longer. I didn't want to get asked that again. At some point, I'd probably let them live until they rotted.

"Do you remember what happened before you died?" the detective asked. I glared, but he ignored me. He didn't show tact the last time I saw him either when it came to letting the victim know they were gone. But I guess that was a good thing. I sure as hell wasn't going to tell him. The zombie hesitated and then seemed to think about it. People said that zombies couldn't think, that they were mindless fragments of the dead, and yet I knew he was thinking. He was feeling what had happened to him all over again. The pain was too much. I wanted it to stop. He was in so much pain. Even though Marcas had an indifferent expression on

74

his face, I could feel how much remembering was hurting him. How could I know that? Was that a necromancer thing? It wasn't like I could ask Jennifer.

"Some guy came in; he was pissed that vampires were on shift. I guess he didn't like it, because he got violent. He wanted to kill Camilla. The others ran away like cowards. So, I tried to fight him off. I'm a werewolf, so I have some strength," he said casually, which made the room pause. It was my first time meeting a werewolf, or at least one that was open about it. I guessed this meant I could raise were-animals as well as humans and pets. Loved that for me. "I wasn't strong enough, because he killed me." The way he smiled as he said that broke my heart.

According to Marcas, the killer fit the same description as the one who killed the groundskeepers. Camilla, rather than being turned into ash like the last vampire, was decapitated. During the conversation, Marcas kept moving closer and closer to me. He held his hand out, and I gripped it in my own. I could feel him relax in my hand. It felt like I was the mother of the undead, even though I very much did not have or want children.

"Why are you holding hands?" Jennifer asked, her arms crossed as she continued her persistent glare. Marcas shot her one back.

"Does it matter," he countered. Ooh, zombies can get sassy!

Jennifer didn't have a verbal response, but her phone was now in her hand. The ferocity of her texting was enough to make me smile. The deputy held out his hand to take it from her. "No cell phones, ma'am." She looked positively livid. My smile widened.

"We have no further questions," Detective Malik said, pointedly looking at me instead of Jennifer. I nodded and turned to Marcas. But rather than being ready, his eyes narrowed.

"What about Camilla? Are you going to tell her community that she's dead? Will she get a proper burial?"

The question seemed to catch everyone off guard. But I was confused, why would it? Of course they should notify next of kin, right? She died. She was also murdered.

"But, she's a vampire," the deputy spluttered, making my skin turn cold. Right. Undead bias was definitely a thing.

"Yeah, and she fucking *died*," Marcas scowled and took a menacing step forward. I quickly gripped his arm.

Malik paused and seemed to consider Marcas's words. He nodded slowly.

"I'll look into her next of kin and see if the community wants to handle the arrangements for her dispos- burial." Malik seemed to catch himself before quickly correcting his own callousness. I wondered idly if he'd actually do it. Marcas relaxed in my grip making me smile in relief.

"You ready?" I asked him quietly. It didn't matter if he was ready or not, but my eyes prickled with unshed tears. Would it ever get easier to put humans back to rest? Marcas's eyes were steady as he looked at me.

"Will you be okay without someone?" he asked and grew tense. His words were so sincere that I was taken aback. Did he want to protect me? I guess he did with Jennifer a moment ago. I was touched. This was the first time anyone had ever spoken to me with such sincerity. What would happen if I told him no? That I had no one in my life, and I would never be okay if I stayed alone. But I knew. I knew he'd ask to stay.

"I have someone," I lied and gave him the warmest smile I could muster. He nodded, and his body relaxed. I wished he hadn't believed me so easily, but it wasn't possible. I could never keep him with me. It was better to let him go. He hopped up on the gurney and laid down with the confidence of someone who knew he was dead. But I could feel his fear. I placed a hand on his forehead and pretended he was just going to sleep. When his eyes closed, his wounds returned, and I was left with nothing. He was just a kid. I guess I never thought about people so young being killed.

Jennifer had already left the room and didn't seem to hear Marcas's parting words. Was she not going to talk to me about how I did? Guess not. Employee evaluations were not a thing, apparently.

"So we've got an MO. Human and vampire murders with consistent notes on how to kill vampires for people who 'need to know,'" the deputy said to Malik which only made the detective narrow his eyes at him.

"She's a civilian and doesn't need to be involved outside of providing us access to the witness," Malik stated, but his detached tone held a hint of irritation.

The deputy's eyes widened as he looked at me, then he turned back to Malik and whispered so loudly that the room next door could probably hear him. "Then why is she here? Why are we raising the dead when zombie testimony can't be used in court?"

Well shit, I didn't know that. Then why was I here? I glanced over at Malik, waiting for him to answer.

"It's a serial killer with a political agenda. We need to get this handled quickly. I'd rather have the answer in advance and find the evidence than us twiddle our thumbs while waiting for evidence that just isn't there," Malik stated sounding a bit tired.

This must have been the same killer too. What was this serial killer's issue with vampires, and why did he have to kill the people protecting them?

I stepped out of the morgue after Malik gave me a pointed look. Obviously I wasn't supposed to be in the room anymore. I released a breath and realized, once again, that I wasn't tired. The last time I raised a body, I was so exhausted it felt like molasses, but here I was feeling fine. I pulled out the totem again and looked at it.

"Are you going to tell me why there's a fully armed guy in the front waiting for you?" Malik asked, making me jump. Armed guy waiting for me? It had to be Rin. But I never noticed Rin being armed. What was he carrying? It couldn't have been guns. Maybe a knife? But then how would Malik have noticed it?

"He's guarding me," I said with a shrug. I hoped he wouldn't ask anything else, but I knew it'd be negligent of him not to.

"From who? You're with the police. Why do you need a guard?" he asked. What was I supposed to say? Some vampire I met said I was in danger, so I had a guard? It's not like anything had happened yet. So this all could be a giant prank. And at what point was I lying to the police? After all, I knew next to nothing. In my defense, I had been kinda busy with a bunch of nonsense, which was why I hadn't pestered Rin too much about all this.

"Just in case," I said with my usual smile. Malik stared at me; his hazel eyes searched for something. I felt my smile falter, but I couldn't give in. If I broke down and told him everything now, it would sound crazy. I didn't know anything anyway. So that wouldn't help him with figuring out how to protect me. It was better to leave it to the people that knew what was going on.

"Fine, but if you need help, I can help you." He was close, so close it was hard to breathe. I could smell cardamom and something rich and dark as he pressed in closer. Was that his aftershave? His cologne? "It'd be better to have someone like me," he breathed the words so softly, I had to lean closer to hear him. Malik caught himself then and quickly stepped back. "Someone who has the law backing him up," he clarified.

I nodded but had no intention of involving him.

"Thank you, detective," I said, creating distance between us and allowed him to escort me from the room. When I reached the lobby, Rin looked pissed. I didn't know what happened, but his frustration was contagious.

"We need to leave," he said with a growl. I glanced at my phone.

"Okay, I've got a raising at the pet cemetery about forty minutes away." His expression told me that's not what he meant, but he grabbed my wrist and dragged me out. The aggression of it was surprising, but I followed. There wasn't a reason not to trust him, so far anyway. Besides, I did have an assignment. Undead, Inc., regularly sent me pet assignments by text. I raised a pet, and they deposited payment immediately.

"Oh wait," I said and screeched to a halt. I ran back inside before he could stop me. "Malik!!! My money," I shouted way too loudly.

The detective was still in the lobby and raised an eyebrow at me as my face grew hot. Damn. I didn't mean to be quite that loud. "Your money has been sent to the office to be distributed to you directly from your employer. I have no cash on me," he said the last bit with a teasing smile. I frowned and tried to hide my embarrassment. Okay, but I seriously needed that money. Rent was due in two days, and here I was with barely enough money to get gas. Not that I needed it since Rin was driving.

Someone pressed against my back, making me jump. Speak of the devil, and he'll cozy up to your ass.

"Are you done? We need to leave," Rin said in my ear. His breath was cool and gave me shivers. I tried to hide it, but I was squirming in place.

"Yeah, that's fine," I murmured as he grabbed hold of my shoulders and redirected me. Malik's arms were crossed, and his eyes narrowed. He was so concerned. Despite his aggressive stance, I could feel that worry. How did I know that?

I forced myself to ignore it, just like how I ignored what I did to Sebastian. I shut it all down. Malik's conflicted protective desires, the frustration of Rin, and the desperation of Marcas to stay by my side, all things that I shouldn't have known.

It scared me.

Chapter 8

"So, what's going on?" I asked. I had already turned on the seat warmer as well as the GPS. Rin's hands were gripping the wheel so tight, I could see the whites of his knuckles. He was livid, stressed, and just a little bit at a loss. I didn't question my intuition. I could just feel what he felt. Breathing was becoming harder. No, if I thought about it too much, then I'd break down. I needed rent money, assassins to stop chasing me, and to find the missing cat first. Once all that was done, then I could take the time to break down.

"The level of threat has amplified," he explained without explaining. I fiddled with my fingers and pointedly looked outside.

"What does that mean?" my voice sounded hollow. I had only just started to calm down, and here I was reminded that my life wasn't my own anymore.

"It means that, for some reason, after the strip club, we now have a new group of people targeting you."

"I don't understand, no one was there outside of that waitress and Sebastian?" I asked and then remembered the priest. "Is the Church of Light going to punish me?" I really didn't think anything could get worse. They *hated* necromancers, let alone someone who just almost killed a guy. Gods, I really, really hoped it was just "almost" and not "did."

Rin sighed and pinched the bridge of his nose as we waited at the red light.

"We need to figure out what's actually going on. I get why the vampire group is after you. They're trying to find something on Hale, and you're the only thing they've got thanks to some stupid good-guy shit he pulled. But this? Whatever you did to that guy is out of my league. We need to figure out what's actually going on," Rin said, then ignored the GPS entirely as he started driving downtown.

"Where are we going?" I asked quickly. I mean, I had time before the pet raising, but not like *a lot* of time.

"Figured we'd go to church. Although since you're a necromancer, you might burn just walking in, but I figure we can find out something at least." Rin was being oddly forthcoming. Maybe he was just as frustrated with the lack of info as I was.

He pulled into the first Church of Light he could find and then threw the gear in park. He turned to me then, his eyes dark and serious.

"We don't know what's happening. But we're going to find out. If I tell you to run, run. If I tell you to hide, hide. If I tell you to shut up, then shut up. There's no negotiating, Lily."

That was the first time I ever heard him use my name. Somehow it made this more serious.

He got out of the car and motioned for me to follow before leading us inside. There was a man at the front counter sorting papers and wearing white robes. As soon as we walked in, he smiled warmly. Before he could speak, Rin held up a hand.

"Earlier, one of your priests came to a strip club when a stripper was hurt. Cuts all over. Is the stripper alive?" Rin asked, not bothering to provide Sebastian's name. I said nothing and stuffed my hands in my pockets.

The man noticed the blood on my clothes and quickly paged a priest.

"There's an injured girl in the lobby with a man who wants to know about some stripper?" He said a bit hesitantly into the phone. I looked down and remembered that, yeah, my clothes had blood on them. Some of it was chicken and some of it was... Sebastian. The thought made me nauseous.

A woman came into the room from a side hallway and smiled warmly at us before holding her hands out towards me. I just lifted my hands and shook my head.

"Oh, I'm not hurt-"

Rin cut me off. "We're here to find out if a stripper that was treated earlier died or not and if you know what exactly happened to him."

The woman paused and looked between us. Her raven hair curled around her face, and she stopped moving towards us. "Yes, we were told of a man who was injured in a club. He's healed now." She spoke the words hesitantly, as though this was privileged information, and she wanted to ensure she didn't reveal too much.

"Okay, so what happened to him? What caused those cuts?"

I half expected Rin to look at me. After all, *I* did it. But Rin acted as though I wasn't even here.

The priestess looked past Rin at me, and her expression softened. She sensed something. I could tell.

"So, you're the little untrained priestess," she said and slowly walked towards me. "Empathy can be a burden. I'm sorry you faced this alone."

I blinked in surprise. What did empathy have to do with this? And why would she call me a priestess?

"What do you mean, empathy?" Rin demanded and took a step forward, cutting the priestess off from me.

The priestess looked confused at first, but then her eyes lit up with understanding. "You're nonbelievers! That makes sense. So, being an Empath is a gift bestowed by the Goddess, which makes you a priestess in training until you master your skills. Somehow you went unnoticed, which is something that needs to be rectified," she explained with a warm smile. "It's how priests and priestesses of the Goddess are able to heal wounds and mend sorrow."

"That doesn't sound like something that would nearly kill a man," Rin pointed out, his eyes dark with irritation at the delayed information.

I'd never healed anyone or made anyone feel less sad unless I made a joke or offered some coffee.

"Right," she said with a sympathetic nod. "Empaths can feel the emotions of those around them, especially when stressed. However, during intense emotions and with an untrained Empath, they may try to protect themselves by throwing the emotion back at the person who caused it. This is where the violence happened. It was initiated against- I assume you, and then you returned the favor, so to speak."

I should have been shocked. I probably was shocked. But in the end, I was emotionally exhausted. That's what made it not matter. So now I was an Empath. Great. The Goddess of Light *hates* necromancers. I'm surprised she didn't just smite me for existing.

"So, do you turn in your own for attempted murder?" Rin asked plainly, as though verifying directions rather than the legality of my actions.

Her eyes widened in surprise. "Of course not! The footage has already been deleted and there were no witnesses. The victim's memory of you is also too distorted to be able to recognize you."

No witnesses? But what about that waitress? Rin's expression didn't change. I guess he was holding our cards tight. Smart. Way smarter than I would have been.

She stepped closer to me, and despite Rin's protective stance, she just knelt down in front of me with a warm smile.

"Priestess-in-training, you're one of us. So you have nothing to fear. Why don't you join me in meeting the leader of this chapel? Maybe we can begin discussing your gift and what it means."

"Oh, no thanks. I'm not very religious," I said quickly and held up my hands. I definitely didn't want to go to church, especially to a church that says necromancers should off themselves since they're abominations.

"Would your organization kill a necromancer? Or an Empath that was 'tainted' by being a were-animal or undead?" Rin cut in. I gasped in surprise. Was he trying to get me burned at the stake? I mean, sure, he mentioned other types of supernatural beings this place hated too, but still. Necromancer was the first freaking thing he listed.

She hesitated, and that was all Rin and I needed to know that the church might be after me too. I wasn't sure they would know that I was a necromancer, but the fact that it was even a consideration that this place might *kill* a being they didn't think should be an Empath was enough to make my skin crawl. This was why I hated church.

When we made it to the car, Rin didn't talk to me until he pulled out of the parking lot and was on the main road.

"You don't seem surprised," he said, his tone even.

"What can I do at this point?"

"It's a lot," Rin said in a voice I think he meant to sound sympathetic but instead came out tired. Given how much attention he'd given to my life, no wonder he was exhausted. "I won't let anyone hurt you."

I looked over at him, but he was focused on the road. It seemed like such a strange promise to make. He was hired to do that already, but when he said those words, it sounded like something more. Rin was sincere. His concern covered me, a suffocating presence as I tried to breathe past it.

My client[26] was pacing in the parking lot of the pet cemetery. I could already tell what kind of person she was. Tall, with a long flowy skirt and a peasant blouse, plus her long light brown hair and giant sunglasses. This lady accidentally killed her pet hamster.

---

[26] Carol (she/her)

"Are you Lily? Please tell me you're Lily," the woman shouted and ran up to me.

"Yeah, I'm her," I said with a smile plastered onto my face. She wanted someone to comfort her and be nice. I wasn't feeling it, but I needed to do this for her.

Hopefully, she'd give me a tip.

"Thank Gods! My name is Carol, and I've got Samantha in this box ready for you," the client said and pulled a shoebox out of her car. She opened it for me, and there in the box was a smushed hamster surrounded by wildflowers. I nodded to her and pulled my switchblade out of my pocket.

"Are you cool if we go ahead and get started?" I asked and took the box from her. Rin was tense beside me, but I couldn't care less about him right now. I had a job, and this was one of the few things I knew how to do with confidence.

I used the knife on my finger and sprinkled the blood over her hamster. The animal was too small for an actual sacrifice. This would have to do. Sure enough, the creature absorbed it and immediately began to *heal*. The hamster sat up and looked at us with its beady eyes.

"Oh my Gods, Samantha!"

I handed the box back and stepped towards the car. I was only supposed to let her have five minutes with the hamster, that's all she could afford, but I usually let it last a bit longer. The dead don't start rotting again until an hour into their raising. At that point, it became more traumatizing to keep it going rather than to let the pet die again.

"You... can raise the dead," Rin said softly from next to me. Fear and horror were coming off him so strongly, it felt like my own. I shrugged my shoulders. You'd think he'd know that by now.

"Not permanently," I pointed out.

"Obviously," Rin said with an eye roll. I smiled at that. So, he knew something about necromancers after all.

"I'm so sorry about the vacuum, baby. I wish I could take it back," Carol sobbed into her hamster's fur as it squeaked. Well then. I wasn't surprised though. Many of these pet raisings were because the pets died by accident thanks to their owners. Expected deaths meant the owners had the chance to say goodbye already.

"I mostly raise pets," I said with a shrug.

"Except when you work with the police."

"Except when I work for the police." I couldn't help a sheepish smile.

I didn't bother telling him that I only just started that gig. I pulled out my phone and checked the bank. A little over three hundred... not bad. But not enough either. I quickly sent the money over to Jazz. I could go another day without food.

"It seems like you're pretty good," Rin continued. I shrugged again. I had no one to compare myself to, so how would I know? I kept glancing at the clock. It'd been longer than five minutes, but not long enough for me to justify leaving. I wanted her to be able to say her goodbyes. And tip. Tipping was important. We stayed quiet and listened to her sobs. I wanted to comfort her if only to get her sadness to stop giving me a headache.

I thought about how raising tiny things was so much easier than big things like people. And then I felt my totem thrum in my pocket. I pulled it out and looked at the weird assortment of hair, bone, wood, and marble.

YouTube had done jack shit for me earlier, so I tried Google instead. There were just articles about famous necromancers with totems and basic details on what to have in one versus not. Then the fact that it's rare. Undead, Inc., totally tried to screw me over with that test. A novice like me should never have been able to create a totem. Totems are a piece of a necromancer's soul. Using it is like making a contract with death itself.

Since google had nothing else to say, I pulled up Facebook. Maybe I'd get lucky and find a group about it or something. Before I could start searching, I heard footsteps approaching.

"Thank you so much for bringing my baby back," Carol said with a forced smile. She handed me the box and started to walk away, but I stopped her with my hand.

"I need to put her back to sleep," I said. She gave me a nervous smile.

"I know. I gave you the box."

"No, I need her body," I reiterated. Great. I wasn't going to get a tip this time. Carol tried to run for her car, but I held out my hand. The hamster jumped out from the woman's pocket and scurried over to me.

"Samantha! Why?! Come back to mommy," Carol shouted, but it was no use. She may have owned her pet before, but it was mine now.

I picked up the rodent and stroked the top of its head while it squeaked happily. I placed it gently inside the box even though zombies couldn't feel pain. "Goodnight," I whispered and watched as it began to decay again.

Carol screamed, and it was full of rage and something beyond sadness. It was as though I was the one who took her baby from her. And I was. I set the box down on the ground next to her as she continued to wail and then turned to go to the car. Rin didn't say anything. I almost wished he would. I wanted to be blamed for her upset. I wanted someone to get mad at me for killing things a second time. The humans were getting to me. I didn't want to look at the face of another human zombie. I didn't want to see the life leave their eyes.

When I got home, there was another note on the apartment door with my name scrawled across it in red ink. The same letter as before. I reached out to grab it, but Rin held an arm out, blocking me. He slipped on some leather gloves and plucked it from the door. I peered over his shoulder to read with him.

Did you enjoy the strip club? Drop the cat case. That is, if you aren't curious what it feels like to be dropped off the bridge of a highway.

My eyes widened. This didn't seem like a prank. Whoever this was *knew* what I was doing. They were watching me. Rin scowled and pulled out his phone. He sent a few brief texts. Within moments, a guy in jeans, a T-shirt partially covered by a grey jacket, and glasses walked up. He had a baseball cap on and ducked his head as he walked through the hallway towards us. Rin passed the note to him without a word. The guy was already wearing gloves as he slipped it into a plastic bag and put it in his jacket pocket.

"So, looks like you've got an admirer," Rin said dryly and opened the door to my apartment.

"So, are you going to look into it?" I asked Rin. The answer was probably obvious but, you know, I wanted to double-check.

Rin just looked at me like I was stupid.

"I take that as a yes. And the person pissy about me checking on the cat probably isn't the group Hale warned me about," I continued, undeterred by his growing irritation.

"Yeah, I don't think a vampire syndicate gives a shit about some cat," Rin said dryly.

"And you said that there was another group after me, and you think it's the church?"

"Have you paid attention *at all*?"

"Kinda. I mean, I've got a lot going on too," I countered and gave him a cheeky smile. It still didn't feel real, after all, no one had actually gone up to me and threatened me outside of Sebastian. So these threats were probably just threats. Rin sighed and pinched the bridge of his nose. I decided to walk past him to get into the apartment.

I got a notification that twenty bucks was in my account. Yay. And yet, not enough. Jazz was on stream in full drag when we walked in. I grabbed Rin's hand, and we quietly snuck past them to get to my room. As soon as I shut the door, I was faced with another dilemma. What was I supposed to do with a man in my bedroom?!

Chapter 9

"So, you can be there, and I'll be here," I said and vaguely motioned to the space next to the bed. My room was practically a closet, and yet, here I was trying to fit Rin inside.

"Why are you acting like a freak?" Rin asked with his arms crossed over his chest. Okay, yeah, I was practically throwing pillows and blankets at him, but I didn't know what else to do. My room was my space, but now I had to share it. If people tried to break in and kill me, it'd be nice to have a guard around. But he was still a guy. Totally not a virgin, but I might as well have been next to this guy. We could be super professional out in the real world, but alone in my room... it felt dangerous.

"You're a man, and you're in my room. How am I supposed to act?" I demanded and ran my hands almost violently through my hair as I looked around my bedroom. I had clothes strewn across the floor, a mess of beauty products I'd never use, as well as textbooks all over the place. I noticed a pair of particularly humiliating lingerie and threw them into my dirty hamper.

"I'm just a guard. Act like I'm not here." He was gorgeous and had the best musky smell ever, and my room was tiny! What was I supposed to do?! How on earth could I ignore him? He made it sound so easy. My face still burned as I grabbed a change of shirt from my dresser.

"Turn around, I'm changing," I said. He held up his hands like I was the police and turned around. One less bra and an oversized T-shirt later, he was good to turn back. I had already shoved myself under my hefty comforter and was hiding my face under my pillow.

"I don't have to be in your room, you know." His smug tone pissed me off. How was I supposed to know this?

"It's too late," I spluttered and motioned for him to turn off the lights. "If you've got nothing better to do, help me find this cat. I've got to find her tomorrow or it won't matter anymore." I already knew this was impossible. The highway was so long, and it'd been days since the cat was tossed. I'd be looking for a corpse. But I needed the money.

My bed was cold. Even colder when he laid down on the ground next to me. There wasn't a lot of space in my room, so he was cramped up against the closet. But even so, I looked at him and wondered, not for the first time, if he was annoyed by this assignment. He was young and attractive. Hale had to have tons of jobs a guy like him could do. What if Rin had a girlfriend? Was I keeping him away from her?

"Go to sleep, idiot," he whispered and closed his eyes. I felt my face heat up as I nodded quickly. Sleep. Sleep would fix everything.

Did meeting Hale in my dreams count as resting? This time we were in a bedroom, but this one was a hundred times the size of mine. The bed had to be king-size and had a thick dark purple comforter. I jumped on the bed and immediately wrapped myself in the covers. In his dreams, things were always fancy. I could feel how soft these sheets were. It was everything I wished I had.

"Glad to see you approve." Hale smiled from the doorway. He was wearing an Evans Blue T-shirt and ripped jeans, very grunge.

"Of course! This bed is awesome. What's the thread count?" I asked and spread out my arms. If this was how I slept each night, I'd always be excited for bed.

"Rin has been doing a good job." My mood soured immediately. "You're here now instead of dead, which is a plus."

I stared at him. Yes, he was trying to protect me. But why? Why did it matter if one girl died or not? Why was it a "plus"?

"I don't understand what you're trying to do. You and Rin both keep saying I'm in danger, and yet the only thing I've seen are two threatening notes about a cat," I said skeptically. At this point, it almost seemed like Rin's main job was to hang out with me and feed me.

I wouldn't have thought of myself as this difficult to kill. If someone wanted me dead that badly, pay my rent and I'd throw up my hands. But this man. He seemed so serious about saving me, when frankly, I had no proof I was in danger. He looked at me then, and I could see fire in his eyes, the kind of flames that could burn a vampire to ash.

"I was informed that there might be a couple groups interested in you. When we went through security cameras at your apartment, we discovered that these notes on your door appeared twice in total. Then, recently, the Church of Light looked into your identity, specifically wanting to know your name, age, occupation, and residence. So initially, when I was only concerned about my rival going after you, I had no idea you were this interesting," he said, the last word a tired laugh.

I ran my fingers through my hair, brushing it back. "I didn't realize I was that interesting either." For a moment, we just smiled at each other, and then Hale seemed to remember himself and quickly straightened up. My chest tightened when he stopped showing emotions. He was so open before, but now the doors were shut tight. I needed to do something to bring him back, to have him open up again. "What are your rivals trying to do? Undermine you? Take over?"

Hale paused briefly as though considering whether or not to explain it to me. Finally, he just nodded slowly as though finalizing some kind of argument in his head. "My competitor doesn't like that vampires are getting so close to having rights, being seen as citizens rather than monsters. Undead Rights is now a term being used by protestors and representatives in Congress. My competitor hates that. He was already against the vampire Church of Eternal Life, and he's definitely against vampires and humans working together. So he has someone killing humans that respect and protect our kind. They started this up northeast but it's much more progressive there, I suppose they thought this conservative area would be different. We only just got vampire supporters to speak out. Texas still has automatic death-row for aggressive vampire crimes. This could exacerbate the issue," he said in a voice that commanded respect.

This felt real, and not only that, this was important to him. As an undead advocate, I easily agreed with his perspective, but I knew humans weren't so understanding. The cops I seemed to be helping more and more were a testament to that. They didn't care about the vampire murders, only the humans.

"I can't believe I told all of that to you," he said and shook his head. I could feel him closing off again, shutting down the connection we were forming. I reached my hand out toward him as though I could physically stop him from shutting me off.

"I'm a necromancer. Of course I'm on your side," I said and reached out to him with my powers. The coldness wrapped him in an embrace that I didn't realize was possible outside of a decaying corpse. His eyes widened as he looked down at his hands. He felt it too. I knew he did. I pushed all my sincerity into the cool embrace of death and prayed he understood me, prayed he knew he was safe with me. His shield dropped ever so slowly.

"You really are one of us," he said and appeared in front of me so quickly it made me jump. He had his hands on the bed on either side of my head as he looked down into my eyes. The closeness was suffocating, and yet, I didn't want him to move, even with his lips barely an inch from mine. He was so sincere. His eyes held me just as much as my power held him. His fingers brushed my hair behind my ear as he kissed me gently on the forehead.

I couldn't stop looking at him, my eyes were so wide. Was this just a thing he does? Kiss girls on the forehead? My face felt super hot, like I had a fever or something, and I was struggling to breathe. What was wrong with me?!

Hale grinned at me and brushed his nose against mine.

"I've never met anyone like you. Determined, kind, an absolute mess, and adorable." He pulled back and looked at my face; whatever he saw there just made his smile widen. "Maybe when all this is done, we can go on a proper date."

My face heated up, but before I could respond, I jolted awake.

Chapter 10

The sun wasn't up, which meant I shouldn't have been awake either. I rolled to my side and looked at Rin. He seemed asleep, but I knew better. My ever-so-vigilant bodyguard. I glanced at my phone and saw a message from Undead, Inc., which said I performed acceptable work at the morgue. Looks like I wasn't fired after all. This didn't seem like the kind of report Jennifer would have given, which made me think back to Detective Malik. It was probably thanks to him.

I also had a message from Jazz with the amount I still owed as well as the past due amount. I knew the number already, but seeing the reminder sent a chill down my spine. I needed that cat. I didn't know how I'd find it, but I needed her. Maybe letting Mrs. Bennett know that the cat was tossed off a bridge would make her pay me anyway before I found the body. I could only hope. Mint began kneading my back, which was cute because cats making bread were always cute. Except she still had claws. I swatted her away as I winced at the latest marks on my back.

"Are you up, then?" Rin asked. He stood up and grabbed some clothes out of a corner. I didn't remember him bringing any, and yet here he was, taking off his shirt right in front of me. I blushed and quickly turned away. He didn't seem to care about me seeing him, but it felt like cheating. Hale and I weren't together though, so didn't that mean checking Rin out wasn't cheating?

"I'm not sure I want to be awake," I said slowly. I felt exhausted. Not only that, but the depression was starting to get to me. First, I needed to tell Mrs. Bennett that her cat was probably roadkill and figure out how much of the pay was salvageable despite this. Then, I needed to check my bank and see if I had anything else I could send to Jazz and Amy before midnight. After that, maybe I could eat something.

Food sounded good. My cramping stomach agreed.

It'd be better to get Mrs. Bennett over with. I hit the call button and waited patiently.

"Bennett residence," a pleasant voice said on the other line.

"Yeah, this is Lily Clarke, I've got an update on Aphrodite," I said groggily.

"Of course! I'll get the Missus!"

There was a brief pause. So brief, I jumped when Mrs. Bennett's voice greeted me. I guess the "Missus" was nearby.

"You found my baby?!"

I cringed. If I could say yes, I'd do it. I'd reunite the two and be done with this nonsense. But instead, here I was with another death I couldn't stop.

"I found the person who kidnapped her," I hesitated. "He threw her off a bridge." The pause felt like it lasted hours. My heart pounded in my chest. I was totally getting fired. Sure, I wasn't the one who killed the cat, but still. That's when she laughed.

"Oh, thank Gods! So, she's not with the kidnapper any longer. That clever girl! I should have put a tracker on her collar," she chattered away. She spoke words. They sounded like they were in English. But I absolutely did not understand.

"Why are you so sure she's alive?" I asked. Out of every death I'd dealt with lately, this was the only one that involved laughter. But I guess that was a nice change.

"Oh darling, I thought I told you! She can't be harmed while wearing her collar, and only I can remove it. It's a brilliant contraption. But I really should have included a tracker. Once you find my darling, I'll rectify this. Keep me updated!" She hung up the phone, leaving me to reevaluate my existence. My cat jumped on the bed next to me and purred. I absently stroked her fur as I looked down at my phone.

"You hear that, Mint? That was the sound of things you'll never have," I told her solemnly. My black tabby just rubbed herself against me more before nipping my hand and walking away. I stuck my tongue out at her pompous ass.

"That collar would have cost around a hundred grand," Rin whistled. I wanted to be surprised, I really did, but here I was in the same situation as before. "You alright?"

I didn't answer and instead grabbed some clothes for the day. While I was looking for a suitable hoodie and leggings, I checked my account. Yeah. It wasn't enough. I shot Jazz the two hundred I made from the police work yesterday and looked at my remaining balance. I didn't even pay a quarter of it. Damn. It was time to get up and make some money. "I've got to make enough to pay Jazz today. So, I guess I'll be figuring that out."

"Strip club is probably hiring."

I threw a shoe at him.

"I'm too fat for that," I scoffed. His eyes widened, but before he could say anything, I left the room to change. Jazz was gone again, which was fine by me. I didn't have time to chat anyway. The cat was probably wandering around and apparently not dying. Posters and talking to strangers were probably my best shots. Damn. When I left the bathroom, I bumped into Amy.

I hadn't seen her in ages, so I hesitated just long enough for her to smile with the charm of both of her dimples. She'd been busy with her residency training, so she was rarely home these days. I smiled back and took in her calmness. As a nurse-in-training, she had a gift for making people feel at ease.

"I heard from Jazz that you were able to pay some rent," she said, her voice gentle. I didn't want to be comforted by this. But I felt hot from pride. I really did pay them something this month. How long had it been since the last time I paid anything? "You look pale, and your lips are chapped. Please don't neglect yourself to pay the bills." I wished I could agree with her and say that I was taking care of myself. But I could count how much food I'd eaten in the last two days. One blueberry muffin.

"How are your clinicals going?" I asked.

"I'm managing."

I was about to say "same" when there was a sudden bang.

The front door was kicked open and three guys in ski masks and all-black attire burst in with guns. As I looked at them, all I could think was that this was a prank. A joke. There's no way. I mean, why would this be real?

Rin immediately entered the room with a gun in his hand and motioned for me to go into the room beside us. Amy reacted before I did; she grabbed my arm and thrust me into her room. She followed me in and locked the door, leaving Rin out there.

My hands were shaking, and I felt cold all over. This was real. I could hear them talking, but it was only muffled voices. I could feel my heart pounding. Amy seemed calm. Her expression a mask of serenity despite everything. I wanted her bravery. But right now, I was waiting to die.

I didn't have to wait long. Gunshots rang out. The shots were in rapid succession. Amy shoved me to the ground. The bullets pierced the walls like paper, destroying Amy's calendar and anatomy posters. She had a picture of the three of us at the beach in Houston. Bullets ruined it. Now I couldn't make out any of our faces.

I trembled. Think. Think. I had to think. But there was yelling. I could hear the door to Jazz's room get kicked open. Ours would be next. Tears streamed down my cheeks. I couldn't remember when that started. Where was Rin? Was he dead? Oh Gods, I killed Hale's bodyguard.

"The window," she said. Right. Escape. We needed to escape. She opened it as quietly as possible. Her window had a ledge. If we jumped down, it was only about ten feet. We could make that. The door behind us was kicked open. I moved to the ledge and jumped before I could think. Amy was already on the ground. My legs almost gave out when I landed, the pain sending a shock through my system.

The moment I touched the ground, Amy was dragging me out of sight of the window as the men began yelling again. Her hand was on my arm, keeping us together and heading in a specific direction. Great, because I honestly didn't care where I went as long as it was away from there. It was all real. Hale and Rin weren't lying.

Were they going to follow us? It seemed like it. Fuck. How were we supposed to escape?

Sirens wailed in the distance. Her hand was on my arm, keeping us together as we hugged the outside wall of the apartment complex. We ducked behind bushes and zigzagged through the complex. I could hear them yelling back and forth looking for us. But the cops would be here soon. They'd stop because of cops, right? Or was this beyond police protection? When we made it to the front office, Amy brought me inside and sat me down in a room away from any windows.

The manager[27] tried to protest, but Amy held up a hand. Her eyes never left my face.

"Lily, I need you to breathe," she said. She had my hands in hers and made me take three more giant breaths. I hated being treated like a patient. But it helped. My heart slowed, and I could think. Amy was talking to the manager now.

"It was my fault," I choked out. Tears filled my eyes as I gripped Amy's hands tighter. I needed her to know that I didn't mean to. I was told people wanted me dead, but I didn't believe it. I mean, not really. There were notes and serious conversations but that's all it was. There were never *guns*. And now I was putting people I loved in danger. I didn't want to put them in danger. Jazz and Amy, their lives were going so well. I was fucking it up.

---

[27] Shelly Massidy (she/her)

"Lily, listen to me," Amy said and pressed her forehead to mine. "You cannot control what others do. People with guns broke in. You didn't hire them, right?"

I shook my head.

"See? And you didn't want anyone to get hurt. I know that about you. You did *not* make bad people do bad things."

I wanted to believe her. The logic was there. But my vision blurred again, and I choked trying to hold back vomit. Amy had me go through the breathing again as police entered the office.

"Are you both from apartment 1110," an officer asked. Amy answered for me. "The gunmen left before we could get here. We have a search team looking for them. I'll need you both to answer some questions for me."

I swallowed hard. But technically, I didn't know anything. I couldn't lie. Amy nodded and moved to follow him, but my stomach hurt and I really really really didn't want to talk to him. My anxiety felt like a blanket, wrapping around me, and I needed it *off,* so I pushed it away. The cop's eyes softened then, and I realized what I'd done. Oh no.

"Actually, I'm sure you girls are exhausted. We'll look into it and give you both some time to rest before we talk again. It's not safe for you to go back to the apartment right now. Do you have somewhere you can stay?"

"We will soon," Amy said quickly, her eyebrows furrowed in confusion at his change of mind. She let go of my hands.

Where would we go? What was she talking about?

That's when a hand rested on my head. I glanced up and started to cry harder when I saw Rin there. He looked unhurt, but his eyes were dark.

I rushed out the door, making Amy reach for me, but I was already stumbling in front of him.

"What happened?!" I asked, my voice didn't sound like mine as I spoke, like something in me broke.

"Your little cat job is really fucking dangerous, apparently," Rin said, his voice harsh but quiet as he reached out to grab my shoulders and inspect me for damage.

"The cat job?" I was so confused until I remembered Aphrodite! Mrs. Bennett's cat! Wait, what?

"Those men were there to kill you since you hadn't told your employer you were going to stop searching."

This made no sense. Why would someone try to off me over a stupid cat that I hadn't even found yet? The look of irritation on Rin's face validated that. I mean, seriously, what the hell?

"Wait, why did you let Amy and I run away alone? I know you were inside but- you obviously knew where I was."

Rin's eyes narrowed as though offended I would ever assume he left me in danger.

"Did you notice how no one chased you?I may not have been next to you, but you were never alone."

I tilted my head. He was so sincere, I could feel his frustration radiating off of him, but also something else. Something sad and self-hating. I started to get lost in his emotions, trying to decipher them when I blinked and realized he didn't know about the police.

"The cops are here. They said we can't go back to the apartment. I have to find somewhere to go," I stumbled over my words, trying to get them all out.

"I've got a place for you to go. No need for your things," he said and flashed my phone, showing he'd grabbed it for me. "Your cat is in the car."

Amy followed me with her phone to her ear and stared at us with her eyes narrowed.

"If I go with you, do you think they won't come after Amy and Jazz? They'll still only target me?" I asked quietly so she wouldn't hear me. Rin looked behind me at my roommate then back.

"I can't promise that. But they will be significantly safer if you're not there." his words came out measured, like he wanted to ensure he didn't lie. I appreciated that.

"Wait, who are you? Where are you taking her?" Amy asked, her eyes narrowed in suspicion. I wanted to tell her the truth, but I couldn't.

"It's fine, I'll go with him," I said. My voice sounded so distant. "Where will you and Jazz go?" I asked her, trying to get past the fog in my head.

"My aunt lives nearby. She won't mind a few extra guests while this gets sorted. But Lily, you should come too. We should be together right now," Amy said, her expression a mixture of hurt and stubbornness. But I just shook my head. If I went with her, then I'd put more people in danger.

"I'll keep messaging you guys. I'll stay safe, so you keep safe too," I said, forcing my voice to sound firm even though I felt anything but that right now.

107

I allowed Rin to help me up as I followed him towards the car. Instead of the black SUV, it was a big white truck.

"We can't keep using the same car. Makes us easy to track," he said simply. I followed slowly, almost mechanically to the truck. Mint was there. She napped in the passenger seat like a queen rather than a refugee. I picked her up and ignored her meow of complaint. I held her tightly to me and breathed her in. She was safe.

As I pressed my lips to the crown of her head, my thoughts continued to race. All of this was real. Someone wanted me dead. They almost hurt Amy and Mint because of it. Gods. All this because of a stupid rich lady's cat.

My phone rang.

"Hello," I said as I buckled myself into the passenger side. Mint was on my lap purring, already comfortable and ready for the drive. She was way calmer than me.

"Lily, what happened?" Detective Malik asked on the other end. "The Church of Light called about an incident involving you and were wanting us to help locate you."

I had a sudden flash of the priest at the strip club. Fuck, they knew. The police would soon know I hurt Sebastian. I couldn't deal with this right now. I needed time. I needed a moment to breathe. I needed anything else. "I can't," I whispered and hung up the phone. "I just can't."

Chapter 11

I was in a loft in Dallas. Apparently, Hale owned a few buildings here. Way way way nicer than my closet at the apartment. The loft was large enough to have a living room, open kitchen, two bedrooms, a bathroom, and an office. But Rin was staying with me in the bedroom without windows. The bed was king-size and looked eerily like the one Hale kissed me on last night. Gods, that was only yesterday. I was hiding under the covers and trying to process everything. That'd be easier if I understood exactly why this was happening.

Amy and Mint almost got hurt, all our stuff was destroyed by the shootout, and here I was in the fanciest place I'd ever been. Unlike Amy and Jazz, I was safe and taken care of. Granted, I guess they were safer without me around. The thought put a shitty taste in my mouth. I never wanted to hurt them.

I rubbed my temples as I tried to think of something, anything I could do to change my situation. Do I just ditch Mrs. Bennett? No longer try to find her cat? And at the same time, there's the Church of Light.

"If you can't help me find out why the church is trying to find me?"

"They want to train you, officially. They sent a pamphlet with the info for the priestess program," Rin said and motioned to the basket by the front door where some mail was. For a moment, I wondered if the mail was mostly addressed to Hale. I threw the covers off of me, making Rin smirk. I guess he'd been waiting for me to come out of my hiding spot.

The pamphlet was everything I didn't want. A glowing yellow, white, and gold brochure with happy faces, all with quotes about how *fun* it was to be a priest/priestess. But then I saw the bottom. It's for kids?

What the hell?

There was even a picture of the Goddess of Light[28] that kids could color in. The Church of Light worships the Goddess of Light. She wasn't exactly known for being forgiving about black magic. Necromancy was definitely a form of that.

"They just want you to come by the church in Dallas and talk to the head honcho there. Nothing suspicious. I can protect you there," he shrugged. But there was a tightness to him. I reached out with the power within me that let me feel others. At this point, that's all I could use to describe it. I was literally feeling him. He was angry. Not just angry, there was rage inside him. The gunmen really pissed him off. I had to pull away. It was too hot, too primal, and too sad.

I understood that anger. I could have lost Amy and Mint. And I only had a few more hours to figure out rent. Why did that even matter at this point? I had a church and catnappers after me. Plus, according to Hale and Rin, some vamps too. Gods, my life was a mess.

"So, we go by the church again?" I hesitated. Rin nodded. I guessed that was it, then. I was going to church. This would officially be twice as many times as I'd ever been to church before.

---

[28] Goddess of Light (she/her)

When it came to religion, there were only two churches. Humans ran the Church of Light. The Goddess of Light established the church. Apparently, she created humans as a show of purity. The people who followed her tended to be zealots that believed humans were supreme. They were very anti-undead and were-animals. Anything outside of humans was trash, and the only way to be forgiven by the Goddess was to choose to die. Which of course meant I was on their die list.

Vampires ran the Church of Eternal Life. Basically, you volunteered for two years, and the church would change you into a vampire. You pay tithe to the church for the rest of your immortal life, but they help you settle and learn how to control your vampire abilities and actively lobby for vampire rights. That one didn't have a god.

The God of Mischief[29] hated churches, so people who followed him had to go without. He'd destroyed just about every altar and building dedicated to him. He cared for all the were-animals. There was a theory that he was the one who created humans' ability to transform. Anything beastlike was in his domain.

Gods were proven to exist. And they had nothing to do with me. Just immortal beings playing favorites. I'd rather play with the dead.

I'd prefer dealing with the Church of Eternal Life. But they weren't the ones putting out posters looking for me. Instead, I had the zealots who wanted people like me dead. I really hoped the Goddess herself wasn't at the church. That'd be too much drama for an already dramatic day.

---

[29] God of Mischief (he/they)

When we pulled into the church, Rin paused before turning off the truck. "Parking lot is all clear, and so are the surrounding buildings," he said. The way he stared at me was so intense. Was he trying to reassure me?

"How do you get all this information? I never see you talk to anyone."

He smiled at me and tapped his temple. "Didn't realize a necromancer could be that slow. Telepathy. We have a psychic on our team."

I'd never met a psychic before, at least not that I knew of. They weren't common, and yet they had shops all over the place. It felt like anyone could be a psychic if they wanted to be. I just never felt the need to look for one before.

Didn't seem all that helpful, what with the shooting we went through. But I guess it was nice to know he wasn't the only one looking after me. Some inept psychic was also lurking in the shadows, I guess.

We stepped out of the truck. The church was a four-story office building. It was white at some point in time, but now it was all grey. The walls had cracks along them and permanent water stains. It was in downtown Dallas, but not the nice part. This was the bit of town that was dying. Everything seemed like it was on the verge of being condemned. I half expected some kind of plaque claiming this place was relevant for some reason or another.

Maybe the Goddess spat on some homeless people here, and now it was a historical marker.

When I walked inside, there was a woman in a long flowing white dress with her hair pulled back out of her eyes. She didn't have any makeup on and had a genuine smile on her face. It was super creepy. I think it's because I was waiting for the Goddess to strike me down. How dare I enter her sanctuary? Or something like that. Maybe she didn't strike people down. That'd be nice.

"How may I help you?" the woman asked. I could tell she was curious about me, but overall, she seemed happy. It weirded me out. Would she grab the pitchforks if she knew I was a necromancer?

"Someone was looking for me. My name is Lily Clarke," I said, which made Rin glare at me. Was that too much info? I furrowed my eyebrows in confusion at him. I mean, the church should know who I am at this point.

The woman's eyes widened, and she immediately grabbed my hands. The warmth that came from her was unreal. Rin tensed beside me but allowed it. I guess she didn't look dangerous. Zealots never did until you were being burned at the stake.

"Thank Goddess you're here! I'll let the head priest[30] know immediately," she said and gave me a wide smile. "He will be so happy you've come." With that, she turned around and ran out of the room. Her speed was surprising given the heels.

"Doesn't sound like they're going to exorcize you," Rin said. I rolled my eyes. It was a relief though. At least one thing in my life didn't seem to lead to danger. A man rushed into the room. He was tall and lanky with light blond hair and hazel eyes hidden behind giant octagonal glasses. He had a

---

[30] Father Abram (he/they)

light tan, and his bony hands were clasped in front of him. But he had a softness to his face that made it hard to distrust him.

"I'm so glad to finally meet you. My name is Father Abram." He held out a hand to me. I tried to shake it, but he just gripped his hands in my own like his front desk lady did.

"Lily, I'm so glad you've come. Can you please follow me? Your friend can come too. I'm sure you have many questions, as do I, so let us talk with refreshments and leisure," he said in a voice that sounded wholesome and otherworldly. Free food and drinks? Answers to my questions? What was this, a fairy tale? He led us up three levels. The church seemed more like an office building, but one of those old-fashioned ones from the '50s. With all the rooms with only a number to distinguish them from each other, it seemed like a white-collar hell.

His office was large and had music playing from his computer. Pop song hits from the early 2000s. Definitely not what I pictured him listening to.

"It's not much," he apologized as he motioned to the coffee machine, a fruit bowl, and a pantry of snacks. I almost cried. My stomach hurt so bad. I hadn't eaten in so long. I stuffed my face as Father Abram poured a cup of black coffee for me. "But I'm glad it suits your taste."

Rin snorted from behind me, but I ignored him. Father Abram's office was full of bookshelves that were filled to the brim. He had natural light coming from his windows with no blinds or curtains. There were a variety of succulents on the windowsill. Wow, he managed to keep them alive. I killed every plant that made its way into my

114

house. He sat behind a large mahogany desk, and the chairs in front were comfortable. They were wooden ones with good cushions.

"So why were you looking for me?" I asked before taking a long drink of coffee. It wasn't too hot, and although black, it had a bit of nutty sweetness to it.

"I saw Sebastian's body and knew immediately what you are. I apologize for not finding you sooner. Normally we find people like us when we are still young, usually in grade school. You are the first untrained adult I've ever met," he said. There was no hint of judgment in his tone. "When our sister church mentioned that you had come by, we couldn't wait any longer."

"Why would you try to find me?"

"Because you're an untrained empath," he said simply. "We don't want another incident to happen, so you must be trained." Father Abram stepped closer to me, his expression soft and kind. He stopped moving then, and I could feel a sense of calm and safety cover me. It sent chills down my spine. This was like what I could do. For me, I thought it was a bit invasive to put emotions on others. So, since Sebastian, I tried to just feel what other people felt. But the priest was using this ability for good.

"Empaths are born and not made. Because of that, our church actively finds empaths as early as possible. There will never be enough empaths. We are healers. Because of this, your existence is incredibly valuable to our church."

"What would you have done if you found me sooner," I asked, but my thoughts were on Sebastian's bloody body. That didn't feel like healing to me.

"We would have trained you. What happened in the strip club was not your fault," he said, his voice soft. I could feel him trying to ease my tension. It almost worked. "Empaths are trained from a young age to control their gift. You have the ability to feel the emotions of others and shift those emotions, and yes, your fear can cause pain. In your case, your ability is powerful enough for that pain to come to the surface. The amount of internal bleeding was much more than I would have expected from someone untrained." He paused then and quickly shook his head. "We don't train empaths to hurt others. It's always possible by accident." Well, that definitely didn't sound good. "But again, the man is completely healed."

"I don't think you will want to train me. I'm a necromancer," I said. I did want training. It'd be nice not to mutilate someone I was questioning accidentally. But when I looked at Father Abram, I knew he wanted more than that. I wasn't going to be a perfect little priestess. Not unless he got cool with a whole lot very quickly. And frankly, the other priestess lady basically agreed that part of the church would want me dead. Obviously not the part that sent out a request to the cops, but still.

Father Abram nodded slowly, then took out a pen and paper. "I had no idea this was the case," he said as he scribbled something down. "And yet, initially becoming a necromancer is a choice, correct?"

I frowned. "Not really. You have to have nearly died, watched someone you love die, and then bleed for the dead. Even then, it doesn't always take. You can unintentionally meet all these conditions, which is what happened to me." I started necromancy at the age of eight, but I didn't feel like telling him that, especially since his religion wanted people like me to off ourselves.

"So, you're like were-animals who were changed by an attack. It was an accident, but there's no reversal," he said and continued to write. I nodded, although I didn't like the way he put it. There were plenty of people who tried to repeat the conditions. It just didn't always work. "I'll speak with my superiors. We may be able to ask the Goddess of Light to reverse your condition. In the meantime, I would like to have you begin training as soon as possible."

Could the Goddess of Light reverse it? Then why did she demand people kill themselves? Besides, I'd been a necromancer for so long that I didn't think I could go back. What would I even do? Be a priestess?

"Lily," Rin said, his voice low. I glanced back and saw him point subtly at the door.

"Awesome. I'll totally be doing that," I said with a forced smile and stood up. If Rin was motioning toward the exit, then it must be time to go. "I'll leave my number with the front desk, and we'll go from there." Father Abram's lips pressed together into a thin line.

"I would prefer we started today."

"I didn't think I'd be here that long, so I just don't have the time," I said and gave a little wave. "I gotta make rent today."

"I'll pay you to stay. How much do you need for rent?" The offer made me stop. What was he doing? Was this a bribe? Could priests bribe people? It seemed a little sketchy. He opened his mouth to continue, but Rin pulled me out of the room and kept leading me until we made it to the front entrance.

The woman was still there by the entrance with a clipboard and pen. She was checking in little kids who were lined up at the door. They had their backpacks on and were chattering among themselves. Gotta indoctrinate them early.

"Can I steal that to write my number?" I asked quietly. She handed over the clipboard without hesitation. It was a check-in sheet, like I thought. Apparently, the munchkins were off to a class about how to have a better next life, and then there would be water balloon fights in the playground. Seemed legit.

"Miss Clarke," Father Abram said from the hall. "Please come again soon." We stared at each other, and I could feel his urgency and concern. It felt so genuine. Maybe he really did care.

"I will," I said and left.

Chapter 12

According to Rin, there was a note on the loft door warning me not to answer the police's call. How did they find me? Was someone tailing us? But if they were then Rin should have noticed, right? Gods fucking dammit. Serial killers, catnappers, and the church were going to be the death of me. Literally. Well, maybe not the serial killer. Hale kept saying he wanted me dead, but he seemed like the only one not bothering with me, which begged the question why Rin was even bothering to protect me since me being in danger seemed to have nothing to do with Hale.

I glanced back at the note. Don't answer the police's call? I had no idea what that cryptic message meant until I was summoned by both Detective Malik and Mrs. Bennett. So, obviously, I ignored the note and showed up anyway. Common sense is a cute idea, but not my forte.

Once again, I was at a graveyard in front of a shallow grave with Mrs. Bennett and Detective Malik. "We have to stop meeting like this," I said with a smile. Mrs. Bennett did *not* smile back. Instead, she dabbed her eyes with tissues as the deputy officer passed me a chicken. Jennifer Caldwell was not amused as she held a camcorder in her hand. Apparently, the office wanted video evidence now. That wasn't terrifying at all.

"So, this was one of your chefs?" I asked and stood over a woman[31] who looked to be in her early sixties. She was Mexican, with long dark hair pulled back and a gunshot wound to the chest.

"Can you make her speak without a tongue?" the detective asked. Uhhh. I knelt by the corpse and discreetly pulled out

---

[31] Alejandra Noriega (she/her)

my phone. Google had ZERO results when it came to making zombies without tongues talk. In fact, there was a Reddit thread about cutting out tongues to keep zombies from being able to be a witness to a crime. Super gross. But it was the only thing I saw on it either way. Great. Jennifer also wasn't giving me any hints with her pursed lips and intense stare. Well, no problem. Fake it till you make it. I discreetly put up my phone so no one else would notice I had used it. Technically we weren't supposed to have phones at crime scenes.

Then again, the only reason this was a thing today was because Mrs. Bennett wanted to know about her cat and paid the police extra to hire me to raise her dead employee. Did she offer hazard pay? Because working for her seemed like a death sentence.

This was my first time seeing a corpse without a tongue. She looked the same as the others except with more jaw damage. All of my zombies went through some temporary healing process whenever I raised them. Maybe she'd get her tongue back long enough to talk to the cops.

"Pretty sure I got this," I said and gave Malik a thumbs up. His skeptical look was enough to get my blood pumping. Sure. I could figure this out. Probably. Besides, this job would get me just shy on this month's rent. I held my totem in my hand, hoping it would keep me from getting exhausted like it did with the werewolf at the morgue. I had checked Instagram before I got here and only found a bunch of pics with crap descriptions, and half the comments called the totems fakes. So Google, Facebook, and now Instagram had failed me. At this point I was going to be stuck looking at Tumblr and Reddit.

With some chicken blood splatter and my trusty totem, I found out once and for all that I could make a zombie without a tongue talk. I guess I needed to add that to my resume. Plus, no exhaustion again. Her jaw temporarily healed, and she was holding her mouth as though surprised to have one. Finally, she looked up at us each individually before acknowledging Mrs. Bennett.

"Ah, Madam, did you like the chilaquiles this morning? I made some for mi marido, but he always forgets to grab it from the fridge," she said and shook her head. Her tongue seemed to be working just fine. So, she was yet another zombie who didn't understand her situation. She looked at me then and frowned. "Chaparrita, you need some food in you, you look too frail." It was so motherly. I found myself smiling at her and shrugged my shoulders.

"I look after myself."

"Not enough, majita. Not enough."

She spoke to me like she knew me. It seemed like all zombies were doing that. It was like we all had this relationship that started on the other side of the veil. Maybe we did.

"Are you Alejandra Noriega?" Detective Malik asked. The Mexican woman stared him down so hard even I cringed.

"Yes, I am Alejandra Noriega. Who are you to ask but not introduce yourself first?" she demanded. Gotta hand it to the detective, his blank expression never changed. He seemed used to this kind of thing.

"Detective Malik. I'm investigating your murder," he said.

"¿Mi ayudas? You can't help me, I'm already dead," she spat. That's when she turned back to Mrs. Bennett. "The chilaquiles? Oh, and I get paid for this too. Give the money to mi hijo, not mi marido. My husband doesn't do enough, and my son is working so hard in school. You give him my life insurance too. I'll be watching you from the other side." The way she said this made chills run down my spine.

"Your food was lovely. And of course, Alejandra. I'll handle everything. I just need to know what happened to Aphrodite first," she said through her sniffles. Alejandra spat on the floor.

"Your gato estupido, she is all you care about. What about your man[32]? No wonder he doesn't like your gato." Oh, so there was a man involved. That was new. From everything Mrs. Bennett told me, I thought Aphrodite was the only love in her life. Alejandra was right. If she had a guy, then this lady obviously preferred her cat.

"Emily Bennett, I will need you to step away during the questioning," the detective said, his tone cold. I didn't blame him. At this point, I was just along for the ride which seemed to include drama and more Spanish than I knew. Mrs. Bennett huffed and stomped away. I was happy to notice her tennis shoes this time. She seemed to have learned her lesson about graves. "What do you remember happening just before your death?"

Alejandra took a deep breath and then glanced at me. Her eyes were so warm, like she wanted to hug me but was holding herself back. She walked to my side with the confidence of a mother. "I finished cleaning the kitchen and went to my car. A man I don't know was talking with someone. I don't eavesdrop, so I tried to leave. They stopped me. Next thing I know, I'm in a trunk. They threw

---

[32] Bram Kenson (he/him)

me in a ditch and shot me. Two men. White boys. Brown hair," she said, her voice cross.

"So you weren't alive when they cut out your tongue?"

Her eyes widened and then she looked at me as though I'd have an answer. I mean, how the hell was I supposed to know?

"They didn't want the dead to talk, but I didn't know what that meant." Wait, did the killers think that if they cut out her tongue I wouldn't be able to raise a zombie that can rat them out? I guess it made sense why Malik was concerned whether the zombie witness would be able to be questioned.

"Can you describe them in more detail?"

"White boys all look the same."

I laughed before I could stop myself. Jennifer and Malik stared at me, but Alejandra was laughing too.

"See, she knows."

"Can you describe the car?"

"Wealthy, black. Not sure. I don't know those logos on cars."

"Approximately what time were you taken?"

"Around 1 p.m."

"Your date of death was approximately three days ago. Were you murdered the same day or a different day from when you were taken?"

"An hour or so later."

"Only two men?"

"Yes."

"Do you remember anything they said?"

"They just hated the gato. We all hate that pompous poor excuse for a cat," Alejandra shrugged her shoulders. I could feel her energy draining. It was starting to sink in for her. "I will come see my family on the Day of the Dead. Do not worry about me," she said softly.

"I know," I agreed and watched as she forced back tears. Zombies shouldn't be able to cry. Although I guess, technically, she wasn't crying yet.

"That is all for now, you're free to speak to your employer."

"I have nothing to say to boss lady. If she pays me for this and takes care of my son, my business is done with her," Alejandra said with a raised chin. I took her hand and led her back toward the grave.

"Wait! I need to know about my cat," Mrs. Bennett shouted and hobbled over to us.

"I told them all I have to tell," she shot back. Then she took my face in her hands and looked into my eyes. "You take care of yourself majita. You are precious. Eat good and live well." The intensity of this moment with her caught me off guard. My mom never did stuff like this with me. She just checked my grades and occasionally asked what I was doing with my life. This felt like what a real mother would say. How she would feel about her daughter.

"Thank you," I whispered. She kissed both my cheeks and gave my face another pat.

"I will visit you too, majita. Leave an offering for me. I don't come for free," she teased. I laughed and held out my hands, releasing the life from her. It was a slow change though. I could see the confidence fall first, and then the strength. Finally, she was a corpse on the ground with no tongue and maggots in her mouth. Despite the visual, I refused to think of anything other than the strong Mexican woman who was just here.

"Mrs. Bennett, I have some questions for you," Malik said, and Mrs. Bennett's face paled. Interesting. I hoped I didn't run into Aphrodite. It seemed like a dangerous meeting.

"Lily, I'd like to talk to you too. Can you come to the station tomorrow at three?" Malik asked. He sounded so polite compared to every other time I'd heard him speak. The way his body stiffened made it seem like he was worried about my answer. But why? It's not like I had a reason to say no.

"Sure thing. I'll see you then," I said and turned to Mrs. Bennett. "Do you still need me, or are you going to do the police instead?" I asked.

She moved forward quickly and spoke so quietly that I almost missed her words. "I don't need you to find out who did it. I just need you to find my baby. The police won't be involved anymore. We were at an agreement of $4,000. I'm going to up it to $8,000," Her eyes had a hint of fury in them, like she finally understood something. I watched her walk away from me, heading to Detective Malik as though nothing happened between us. Was it even possible for me to find her stupid cat at this point? And would I die before I found her? If these notes and the gunmen were any indication, I'd probably be dead before ever seeing any other kind of assassin. The money seemed more and more like a pipe dream.

Surprisingly, Jennifer was the next person to walk up to me. "The office will call to schedule a meeting with the executives regarding your performance so far," she said. Although she tried to keep a straight face, her eyes glittered. Obviously, she had been talking shit about me. Great.

"Looking forward to it," I beamed at her. Sure, she was a bitch. But there's nothing bitches hated more than a positive attitude.

I headed toward Rin. His annoyance was so intense I could feel it from the grave.

"No attempts?"

"None. That doesn't mean you should go out on every job you get." Rin scowled.

"You seem to be forgetting that I'm broke as hell."

"If you need money, Hale would probably give you some. How much do you need? Five thousand? Ten?"

I stopped.

"Seriously?"

"What, you saw where he set you up, and you still assumed he didn't have the funds?" Rin asked.

"Yeah, but why would he offer any to me?" I countered, but it didn't actually matter. I never asked for money as a general rule. "It's fine. I don't have the kind of consistent money where I could pay him back anyway. So, these odd jobs are going to have to be my ticket out of debt for a bit."

"And an early grave. You're just throwing yourself out there for assassins, you know."

"Maybe, but wasn't I in danger from the start anyway?"

He said nothing. Probably because I was right.

Chapter 13

I was one dead body away from paying rent. Unfortunately, I was still kicked out, but at least it wasn't my fault.

"I'm sorry, Lily. I know shit hit the fan. But the apartment is destroyed, and we don't feel comfortable going back. Amy said you've got a friend that's helping. If you can stay with them while you're getting these extra jobs with work, you'll be fine," Jazz said on the other line.

"What about you two? What are you doing? Did you find a more permanent place to stay?" I asked, genuinely wanting to know that they were safe.

"I'll be rooming with my drag friends, and Amy is staying full-time at her residency now. We'll be okay. We're just worried about you," they said, making me smile softly.

"I'll be fine. I've got some people helping me get on my feet." This technically wasn't a lie.

"Thanks, Lil. I know it's been rough lately. But you've been getting it together. I think you're on your way," they said.

"Yeah, I think so too," I said while curled up in my blanket again. There was this thing called getting out of bed. Yeah, that wasn't going to happen for a while. I checked my bank account and couldn't help a small smile of relief. I did get some money from both the police and Mrs. Bennett for the raising. She even tipped despite Alejandra not wanting to talk to her much.

Mint curled up with her ass in my face. I immediately rolled over. "I'll check in later. Keep me updated, okay, girlie," Jazz said. Their voice was soft, as though they felt bad too. Good. At least I wasn't the only one that felt like shit.

I made a small sound of agreement and then hung up. Although there wasn't much of a rush, I still needed to pay them back. The only way to do that seemed to be working with the police. Murder victims everywhere. It didn't seem like life was going my way. Granted, dead people meant I got paid. The callousness of that thought didn't make me feel any better. It was only noon. I still had three hours until Malik wanted me to drop by. How long was that supposed to take? What did he want to know? I really didn't feel like talking about all this stuff I didn't even understand.

Couldn't he just give me another dead body?

"I've got Chinese," Rin said from the doorway.

"I didn't order any," I grumbled and tried to muffle the sound of my growling stomach.

"I did. When you don't eat, I don't eat. I'm hungry, and we have Hale's credit card," he said with an upbeat tone of voice. I opened my mouth to ask if that was really okay, but then he pushed sweet and sour pork in my face. Well then. I mean, it's not like I could say no to that. Besides, it was kind of insulting being called out for being too broke to buy food. I was having to rely on someone else's charity. Or stolen credit card.

"I guess I'll eat some, but I'm protesting inwardly," I said.

"I have crab rangoons in the bag," Rin said, motioning toward the small brown bag in his left hand.

"No more protesting," I said quickly and held out my hand for it. He laughed, and it was such an odd sound coming from him. We both ate in silence on the bed. It wasn't uncomfortable. If anything, it felt nice not to have to prove myself to him. It seemed like most people I'd been around lately expected something from me. For the most part, Rin didn't seem to want anything. Outside of me staying alive. That was turning out to be much harder than expected. But at the end, didn't my wants matter too?

For a moment, I just thought about everything. I had been compartmentalizing for so long. But at some point, I needed to look at the full picture. I pulled out a notebook and took bites of my sweet and sour pork while writing down what I knew.

Aphrodite was a death wish. I really needed to drop the investigation. The money sounded good, but why the hell was I risking my life over finding some rich lady's cat?

I still had no evidence that people were actually after me because of Hale. Part of me figured Rin was just around to keep tabs on me. Maybe Hale wanted my powers, like the necromancy thing and maybe now the empath stuff too. For a rent-free loft, I was kind of cool with being used for my powers. Probably.

Then there was the Church. One priestess admitted that parts of their organization might want me dead because I'm a necromancer as well as an empath. That's blasphemy on so many levels. But Father Abram was pretty nice. Not that nice meant he wouldn't kill me, but it was definitely a point towards it.

Being an empath was a new thing. I had no idea what it meant. I mean, empaths are supposed to heal people and take away pain, but here I hurt someone. Why did this ability never come out before then? The more I thought about it though, the more I realized that I had been feeling it. When I was around people. I kept sensing emotions I should have had no idea about. It wasn't all the time, but when I was stressed, I could feel it. I didn't want to hurt anyone else.

"I want to be trained on how to be an empath," I said to Rin, making him choke on his General Tso's chicken. He had to down some water as he looked at me like I was crazy. I probably was. I mean, it's not like this would happen to a *normal* person.

"The church hates necromancers," he pointed out with narrowed eyes.

"Yes, but they said there aren't a lot of empaths. Maybe I can use that to my advantage. Besides, if I let Malik know I'll be trying to have the church train me and they know too that the police are aware, wouldn't that give me some form of protection? Like, they can't exactly kill me if a detective has me on call." I was probably being naïve, but I didn't care. I was tired of people making choices for me.

"Hale isn't going to like this," Rin said and set his chopsticks down. I frowned, and then realization hit me. He's paying for the loft. The place I'm staying. What if he revokes it because I want to do something he doesn't like? Fuck.

"Can you let him know that I'm willing to use my ability for him in exchange for room and board?" I asked quickly, willing to barter my powers for a place to stay. If he really paid for my housing and food, then I could save up for school. I could get my degree in preternatural studies and stop being an intern. Jazz had called me out for not pursuing my degree anymore, and now I might finally have a real shot at doing it. It would be a pay and status increase. I could finally be a real necromancer. Someone with actual training rather than just Google.

"I'll talk to him, but this should be done in person," Rin said. His tone was even now, as though I'd crossed some kind of line.

"Can I meet with him, then?" I asked. Rin shrugged his shoulders, but he wasn't looking at me anymore. Guess not. "How close is he to dealing with the reason for the assassins?" This question was met with more silence. I didn't even get a nonchalant gesture. I sighed heavily and put down my food. I wasn't hungry anymore. "For now, I might as well get ready to see Malik. You gonna be cool with me going to the police station?"

Rin gave a heavy sigh but didn't say no. I must have pissed him off or something. He wasn't acting like normal. So, I decided to test it out. I would find out what he's feeling for sure. I closed my eyes and thought about Rin next to me. Nothing happened for a few moments, and then I could feel it. He was scared, angry, frustrated, and at a loss. I couldn't tell the reasons for it, emotions weren't like that. And honestly, when were emotions logical? But right now, I wanted to help him relax. I wanted him to breathe. But even though I wanted this and tried to will it into happening, nothing changed.

This was why I needed the church to train me. I didn't know what the hell I was doing.

"So, the police station first and then maybe go to the church?" I asked hesitantly. Currently, he was my ride, and I was dead broke. But if he refused, I'd probably drag Jazz into this for a ride. Except that'd probably be stupid and dangerous given the fact that people were after me. I decided to pass the time by going to a coffee shop across from the loft. People filled the cafe to where all the tables and couches were occupied. Cool, so I guess I was just gonna walk in and out. Rin walked in behind me and looked around in distaste.

"What's your deal?" I asked him with raised eyebrows but he just scowled.

"Did you seriously not notice? Everything here is gluten free and vegan. Trendy bullshit."

I couldn't help laughing at him. I accidentally caught the attention of an employee with the nametag 'Jamie' and quickly looked away.

"You do understand that some people have allergies right? And morals?" I hissed under my breath, trying to get him to understand without bringing too much attention to ourselves. He gave me an incredulous look.

"You *kill* animals to raise the fucking dead and you're lecturing *me* on the morality of being vegan?"

I blushed and got into line. "I mean, I'm not vegan, but some people do it because they-

"Don't kill chickens with their bare hands and a knife?"

I glared at him but it didn't come out as harsh as I'd like because people were looking at us now. I ordered a super sweet drink in the hopes of getting rid of the sour taste in my mouth.

Rin just ruffled my hair and got a cold brew with a quad showing me, once again, that he might be crazy.

"Are you ready?" he asked. I nodded, then remembered Jennifer had said something about a performance meeting, but since I hadn't gotten a message about it, I decided to shrug it off. Not my problem until someone gave me a time and date. I had plenty of other crap to worry about.

I checked my email just in case and cursed under my breath. Yeah, they totally sent me a meeting time and date. It's today. Dammit.

Sure enough, Rin wasn't allowed into Malik's office. I expected as much. But Rin said that the station was being heavily guarded from the outside. So, I guess that meant I was probably safe.

Malik had nothing on his desk. There was a large and intimidating file cabinet behind him, then his desk with almost nothing on it except a notepad and pen, plus computer. Everything looked organized. Way more than my place. If I were a detective, my office would be a wreck. There would also probably be some kind of giant whiteboard full of useless information. I saw it on TV once. Instead, his office looked like not only would there be no evidence if he committed a murder, but he'd have an alibi with witnesses and character references.

"You've had an eventful week," he said and pulled out a file. I could see my name on the tab. I guess he would be checking up on me from now on. That didn't seem like a good thing. The file was also significantly thicker than I wanted it to be. "The background check on you was extended to cover more ground. You are the youngest to become a necromancer ever recorded. Do you know why it started when you were so young?" Oh. Is this all he wanted to talk about?

"I really don't remember much about back then. But yeah, I know I was young. Didn't do much more than roadkill raisings though," I said with a shrug, not really minding talking about this. I had totally thought he was gonna bring up Sebastian. Or maybe the shooting in the apartment. Or even the fact that the Church of Light wanted me now.

"What about the girl? Your friend from the car accident," Malik continued. I looked at him, confused.

"I've got no idea what you're talking about."

"A neighbor girl was the first thing they ever recorded you raising. It's how your necromancy was discovered," Malik said slowly, his eyebrows furrowed as though trying to see if I was lying to him on purpose.

I definitely wasn't lying. How could an eight-year-old raise a human from the dead? That's insane.

Malik made a note in my file, then looked up again. This time, his eyes were intense, like he knew I'd be defensive about this bit. Fuck.

"Do you want to explain why you have a bodyguard? And why was your apartment broken into and shot up? And why is the church looking for you?" I knew my rights well enough to know that I didn't have to answer him. It probably wouldn't help our working relationship, but I also didn't really have an answer for him.

"Are you interrogating me?" I asked with a forced laugh. Malik didn't laugh. He didn't even smile. Instead, he leaned forward with his hands folded under his chin.

"Should I be?"

Oh Gods. I swallowed hard and tried to think of a way out of this. It's not like I committed a crime. Well, except that thing with Sebastian, but that was totally an accident, and a priest took care of it afterwards.

"Kinda crazy how you want to know all about me," I said, my voice raising way too high as I smiled a bit nervously.

"I took a risk and hired you to help with my investigation. I need to make sure my trust is well-placed," he explained firmly. It was so reasonable, I felt bad for hiding what was going on. Maybe I could explain a little? Just enough so I didn't sound completely crazy?

"He's just protecting me, just in case something happens. I mean, I'm a necromancer and an empath, so the Church of Light won't like that. Plus, I'm helping with your serial killer case," I explained. He looked at me evenly.

"I never said that case was a serial killer investigation."

"Yeah, but it's like the same MO, and I heard your officer guy say you keep getting notes about how to kill vamps with each of these double homicides. Why wouldn't it be a serial killer?" I asked, perplexed by his avoidance.

Malik leaned back in his chair. "There is a possibility that it's a serial killer, or it could be an organization, or a copycat. There are no clear answers currently."

I blinked in surprise. Oh. And here I thought it was obvious. Okay then.

"Why aren't you seeking police protection for these threats you're facing?" Malik asked, his tone implying that I could be lying. Thanks for the vote of confidence.

"I mean, it could just be in my head," I said quickly, rolling with the idea that I might just be crazy. Didn't seem too far off, honestly.

"I see."

I did NOT like the sound of that *I see*. Malik didn't say anything when he stared at me. His brown eyes seemed to be looking for something. Whatever it was, he didn't find it.

"We're done," he said with such finality, I paused.

"Working together too or just this conversation?"

He finally cracked a smile. "Just the conversation." I sighed in relief, then gave him a wave as I quickly left the precinct.

Chapter 14

Before I could go to the church, I had to meet with Undead, Inc. This time, I was meeting the execs at their headquarters in Fort Worth. It seemed silly that in the middle of the Stockyards, cowboy central, there was a three-story building where all the higher ups at Undead, Inc., worked.

The front desk had two people, both of whom were on the phone.

"Ma'am, I have explained repeatedly that we cannot bring back your dead turtle. We've already raised him eleven times. Our necromancers have made it clear that your pet is unable to be raised again," the male receptionist said with a voice that was becoming higher and higher in pitch.

"Does Tuesday the 30th at 8 p.m. work for you?" The female asked. Her phone call seemed to be going much better than his.

He slammed the phone down, abruptly hanging up on the client, and turned to me. Was there a polite way to ask to wait for the girl to handle me instead?

"Client or intern?" he demanded.

"Intern." Damn he sounded mad.

"Appointment?" At this point he wasn't looking at me anymore and instead had his eyes glued to his computer. He had copper skin and thick black eyebrows. His scowl must have been contagious, because Rin's face mirrored his.

"Yeah, for Lily Clarke," I said hesitantly. Was he going to yell at me? But no, he just pointed to the stairs. "Top floor.

They're waiting for you in the conference room. You're five minutes late." Of course, this was when the woman's call ended. She smiled pleasantly at me, but it was too late.

I sighed and climbed up the staircase. If he was pointing out my tardiness, then the executives probably noticed too. Although I'd been eating lately, I felt a bit lightheaded going up the stairs. Calories were still hard to come by, and burning them wasn't the greatest idea.

When we got to the third floor, there were only three rooms. One of which, the conference room, was right next to an elevator.

"That bastard," I gasped.

"Yup. Bastard," Rin agreed.

I scowled. We were totally taking the elevator back down. I knocked on the door to the conference room. I could already see Jennifer through the glass. She was sitting there with Chae-Won, Karen, and Joseph. Of course, Joseph was the one to let me in. I gave him a nervous smile and quickly sat down in the chair across from them. Rin stood by the exit.

"This is a private meeting," Jennifer said with narrowed eyes.

"I'm her bodyguard," Rin said with such force that I flinched. Damn, sir. You didn't have to go that hard.

"That's fine. In this line of work, there are people who can become violent when we put their loved ones back in the ground," Chae-Won said, her voice quiet but firm.

The silence after was awkward, but luckily, it didn't last long. Karen gave me a wide smile that almost looked sincere. "So, you've raised two bodies for the police so far, not counting the one that wasn't authorized. How would you rate your performance?"

It took me a second to realize what they were talking about when Karen suggested one of my zombies was unauthorized. That's when I remembered Ricky Baun, the gardener. Right! I had only gotten paid as if it were a cat case. I wondered if maybe I could get back pay on that, but this didn't seem like the greatest moment to ask.

"I'd say I've done pretty well," I said and tried to sound confident. That would be easier if my voice didn't break when I said the word "well."

"The Preternatural Investigation Unit has commended your work," Joseph said. The chill of the room warmed up some. I leaned back in the rolly-chair and took a deep breath as discreetly as I could. Thank Gods. It definitely seemed like Malik liked me well enough, but the confirmation was nice.

"But that doesn't mean you've passed with us," Jennifer said, her smirk in full effect. I hated her more and more.

"The concern is more about how you completed the raising. You taking on a human case as an intern is a legal issue for us. Had it gone wrong, it would have cost the company in fines and lawsuits," Chae-Won said, then gave Jennifer a pointed look. "However, there are some accomplishments we need to acknowledge. According to our colleague, you have raised the dead outside of a graveyard, during the day, and had an undead regain her tongue when animated. As well as all this, your raisings have produced undead which appear lifelike with zero signs of decay."

Well, when she put it like that, it sounded impressive. But really, I was just doing what Google told me to do.

"Should I have done it differently?"

"Do you know how to do it differently?" she countered. My frown deepened. She got me there. Was this the time to admit I had almost zero training?

I reached out with my empathy to try to feel out what Chae-Won felt about this. It would have been more convenient if I could read minds rather than emotions. She was nervous and also confused. I tried to search deeper but couldn't figure out what the other emotions were. Chae-Won didn't seem to notice what I was doing, which was great since I didn't know exactly what I was doing either.

"So, you're inept," Karen said with a harsh laugh. It took me a moment to realize she wasn't talking about my attempt at using my empath ability, but rather, my ignorance about being a necromancer. Great. Jennifer and Karen could be best friends at this point. They had so much in common. Mostly that they both sucked.

"Her talent obviously says otherwise," Joseph said. I had newfound respect for him.

"Yes, I believe she can continue to work with the investigation unit," Chae-Won agreed. Her expression was indifferent, but she acknowledged me, so she couldn't have been anti-me like the other two women.

"But she obviously lacks training," Jennifer cried.

"And yet, she's a better necromancer than you," Chae-Won pointed out. Damn, the tension was high in this room. Jennifer scowled, her face bright red as she refused to look at me. Her anger was palpable, and yet, I couldn't help relaxing. I could keep my job for a bit longer. "This is it for our meeting today."

"Okay," I said. "See you later!" Jennifer did not share my enthusiasm, but who cared? I passed!

I raced after Chae-Won before she could fully leave the building. Rin had to jog to keep up and looked extremely irritable about it, but I didn't care.

"Hey, can I ask a question?" I asked her with a tired smile and waved my totem.

She just stood there staring at me. It took me a moment to realize she was waiting for my question. Right.

"Um... so what's a totem do?"

The look she gave told me she regretted advocating for me in the meeting. She said nothing and walked away as though I were a bug. Fun. So, I still didn't know what a freaking totem actually was.

Chapter 15

When we finally got to the church, I was drained. Father Abram gave me the warmest welcome I'd ever received in my life though. There was coffee, a full dinner, and an assortment of notebooks I could choose from for what was apparently going to be my emotional diary. I needed to understand my own emotions before I could fully understand others. It was a bit childish, especially when I opened one and found coloring sheets explaining the different emotions, complete with stick figures with various expressions.

"I apologize; the study materials are normally given when an empath is young. We haven't made any that are suitable for adults. Once you learn the basics, then there is adult material you can use for reference," he said with an apologetic smile. I shrugged. It wasn't the first time I was treated like a child. Besides, coloring when I was bored didn't seem so bad. It'd been ages since I colored anything.

"So, I'm supposed to read people's feelings based on the sensations," I asked and held up a picture of thorns, water, snow, and sand. Rin was watching us closely from the side of the room. He had a hand on his belt as though there was some kind of weapon there. Whatever it was couldn't be too big.

"Yes, right," Abram said and took the page from my hand gently. It was such a timid gesture coming from a man so tall.

"Everyone feels emotions differently. This is especially the case with empaths. Each emotion has a specific texture to us. It's something we're familiar with within ourselves. It's harder for us to acknowledge when others have a similar texture, though. This is a visual way of understanding that, as well as determining words for what you believe these emotions feel like to you."

On the table, Father Abram had put bowls with the different objects inside them, literal bowls of sand, water, ice, and thorns. I wasn't exactly in a rush to touch the pointy bits.

"Normally, empaths get sucked in by the emotions of those around them and think those feelings are their own," he continued. "But for you, you seem to understand they aren't yours. Do you know why that is?"

This didn't sound like the kind of question he had the answer to. It's not like I knew either. I just could feel a thing and knew who the actual feeler was. But the way he said it made me think about it more. How did I know?

"I think my emotions are muted," I said slowly. I refused to look at Rin as I said this. It felt oddly vulnerable. "If I feel, then it's detracting from others." I had a quick flash of a memory with me and my parents. I was crying over something, and they just... It wasn't a good thing to feel. You'd get punished.

Father Abram took a deep breath, then placed my hand in his own.

"This will need to be a longer discussion. For now, I want you to try to check in with your own emotions." When he released my hand, I caressed the different objects gently. Did feeling really come out this strong? Was I weird for just... going with it?

He gave me three worksheets; each one was an emotional competency test. Basically, I had to read a sentence about someone and write down what emotion I thought they would feel based on the scenario. It came with pictures you could color in. I half-expected him to hand me a box of crayons to go with it.

Once I was done, he graded it in front of me and then went through the ones I got wrong. Not a lot, but enough to make me feel dumb.

Rin never stopped looking at me, which was creepy enough as it was. But I guessed he had psychics watching outside. Still, I could feel a sense of calmness from him. It helped me breathe.

"I talked to the higher-ups about having the Goddess remove your necromancy. It will be brought up with her the next time she visits one of our churches," Father Abram said cheerfully, as though he was talking about something typical, like an upcoming barbeque. Were gods that easy to get ahold of? Jeez.

I still didn't have the guts to tell him that I'd rather not lose my powers. Necromancy had been part of me for so long, it'd be like losing who I was in the process. Even so, I just nodded at him and worked on the next sheet, which, of course, came with an assortment of forty-eight crayons. I was supposed to color what I thought each emotion was on the page. I had officially become a child. Great. Just give me a dead body, and I'd be out of here.

Chapter 16

I shouldn't have been so cheerful about murder victims. This time, I was looking at twins. Apparently, one twin was a vampire and the other a member at the Church of Eternal Life. She[33] hadn't been at the church long enough to be changed, but her brother[34] had. Unlike the last two vampire kills, this one was staked through the heart.

"Isn't it weird that the vampires keep dying in different ways?" I asked. Malik gave me a look but didn't say anything. I guess I wasn't supposed to give an opinion. Is that why they were saying before that the killer kept leaving notes on how to kill vamps? He did it while also showcasing how? That's super fucked up.

Chicken blood and my totem were becoming so common for me now that I didn't even notice until I was splattered in blood and had the totem thrumming in my hand. Even the act of the chicken dying was too swift for me to recall doing it. My apathy was probably getting dangerous. "Might need a vacation after this one," I muttered. Then again, with all the back rent I owed, I still needed the dough.

"I'll give you a vacation when I get a vacation," Malik said. His eyes were bright as he leaned against the wall of the morgue.

"Yeah, but you seem like the type that doesn't take those," I countered. His deputy laughed. He had a light beer gut and big brown eyes. He reminded me of a deer with his light brown hair and defined cheekbones. It seemed silly to have so much definition on someone who looked like Bambi's

---

[33] Dorothy Cannon (she/her)
[34] Damon Cannon (he/him)

dad. Malik gave him a look akin to a disappointed father, then turned back to me.

"Are you ready?"

I looked down at my bloody hands, then shrugged my shoulders. I flicked the blood over the body. Jennifer wasn't here this time. It didn't seem like a good thing to me. I figured someone at Undead, Inc., would let me know if I was approved for solo missions. Her not being here was probably more to do with Malik than my skill. He seemed to really hate her.

The victim was in her early thirties, a bit older than me, and had worry lines on her face. When her eyes opened, she immediately looked over at her brother and stifled a cry.

"So, Damon and I really did die," she said and reached her hand out toward the body of her twin next to her. I took hold of that hand and tried to make her feel at ease.

But really, how could you make anyone feel better knowing they and their other half died? Even so, I tried. She felt cold, like snow. I only knew this from Father Abram's lesson. This must be the feeling of losing someone that close. I couldn't figure out how exactly to melt it, but I did seem to do something, because she relaxed her shoulders.

"Are you Dorothy Cannon?" Detective Malik asked. She used my hand to help her sit up from the floor. She had short blond hair that was almost white in appearance. She was a bit on the heavier side, with a round face. Her clothes were caked in her brother's blood. Her cause of death seemed like strangulation before the raising, but now her neck looked fine.

"I'm Dory," she nodded and leaned on me. It was another overly familiar gesture from the undead. Unlike the others, the murder happened outside of work. The two were staying late at the Church of Eternal Life when a vampire broke in and targeted them. The other members were in the main office while Dory and her brother were setting up the pamphlets behind the chairs in the chapel.

"Can you tell me what happened before you died?" the detective asked. It was a standard question at this point. I could have given the interrogation with how many times I'd heard it. And yet, Dory looked at me instead of him.

"Well," she said as though she was waiting for some sort of direction. When I didn't respond, she rolled her eyes. "What am I allowed to tell him, and what am I not?" Well shit. Way to make me look sus.

"I don't know why you're asking me that," I said and held up my hands. "Just answer his questions so he can catch your killer." Dory rolled her eyes again and shook her head.

"The priest was talking to us about how we needed to prepare for a new priestess with the Church of Light. Basically, we all needed to be extra wary because this girl was up to no good and would be going after us. Then he showed us a picture of you. He said you had to die," she said and motioned towards me. My mouth dropped open. What the ever-living-fuck was this?

The Church of Light was acting friendly now, but being a necromancer put a damper on me becoming any kind of priestess. Why was the Church of Eternal Life involved? The two churches had nothing to do with each other.

How was I supposed to handle yet another threat to my life? Rin had his work cut out for him. Maybe Hale wouldn't bother to protect me from the dangers of my own making. I wondered if I could be allowed my phone to text Rin that there was another group that wanted me dead, but at the same time, I just wanted more info. I had to get more.

"Did he say why I was such a threat?" I asked, but Detective Malik shook his head at me.

"I'm the one asking questions," he said. Whelp. Damn.

Dory didn't seem to get the hint. Instead, she spoke earnestly. "He said you were a necromancer and that necromancers shouldn't be priests, but if the church makes an exception for you, then it's no good. He made it sound like the church needed to get rid of you. A necromancer empath could potentially control vampires." At this point, her eyebrows were furrowed, and she seemed to be getting lost in herself. "Anyway, when he was done talking to us, he left to go meet with someone. I don't know who. My brother and I always help prep the chapel, which is what we were doing. A man came in. He was really angry. He thought more people would be here, but he got the time wrong. There was just me and my brother. The rest was quick. I think I died first," she said and looked toward her brother again. I wanted to say something, try to keep her calm or to help her feel better in general, but it wasn't going to work. I knew it already. I don't know what I would have done in the same situation. My brother was still safe in high school. But imagining him dying hurt. I guess it was a blessing she died first.

"What did the killer look like?" the detective asked.

"Tall, tattoos all over. The tattoos looked like words, but I couldn't read them."

"Was he alone?"

"Yeah. He was super powerful. I've never seen anything move that fast. He also said he needed to get to someone. She was next or something. I don't know. I'm not sure anymore," Dory said, her eyes darting to her brother. I put my head on her shoulder and took several deep breaths. Me being calm seemed to calm her down too. "I think he worked with Jareth[35]."

Well, that was a new piece of information.

"Who is Jareth?" Malik asked.

She stilled against me, but then she looked at her brother again and something changed. "We're dead, it doesn't matter anymore. Besides, I think this will help you." She turned to me with an intensity in her gaze that no undead should be able to possess.

"There's a struggle right now between a Master Vampire named Hale and a Master Vampire named Jareth. They each want to control this area. Jareth wants to get rid of vampire and human relations. Hale likes the way things are progressing. I think Jareth ordered this attack. Jareth hates our church, but Hale doesn't mind us, so we support him. We aren't supposed to talk to the police about it because murder is against the law, but one of them has to die for the dispute to end."

"Where can I find this Jareth?" Malik continued.

I was still caught up on Master Vampires. They were able to subject other vampires to their will and possessed a tremendous amount of power. The fact that I was in an

---

[35] Jareth (he/him)

ambiguous relationship with one seemed a lot more frightening now.

"I don't know. The church might. We try to avoid him, but I died, so I guess we didn't do a good job," she said, her voice began to tremble.

"I don't know how much longer she'll last," I told Malik. He nodded.

He asked a few more questions about what Jareth looked like and where someone could look for his followers, but Dory was no help. She gave a relieved sigh when I allowed her to die a second time. I only loved the money from necromancy. I hated watching people die.

"We need to talk," Malik said and motioned with his head for the deputy to leave the room. When we were alone, he stepped so close to me, I could smell the spices from his aftershave. My breath stuttered as I tried not to pay attention to the feeling of his breath on me. Why was he so close?

"What are we talking about?" I asked, as though I didn't already know.

"There was a shooting at your apartment and now there's a witness saying that two churches are potentially after your life."

"Okay," I shrugged.

"Okay? That means you're in danger."

"I told you as much yesterday."

He gave a heavy sigh. "Yes, but is your bodyguard protecting you from the church or someone else?" he asked. It'd be a crime to lie to him, right? Something like obstructing or whatever.

"I don't know. I mean, I'm on this dangerous case with you, and I just found out I'm an empath. And frankly, the Church of Light made it pretty clear that necromancers should die," I said casually, my emotions just not sticking around for some reason.

"You really won't talk to me," he said and stepped back. He frowned. It was like I hurt his feelings. Did I? Could I? To have someone that handsome care about me was a bit odd. This was the third hot guy that cared about me since I raised a human for the first time. I mean, not saying the two are related, but it was definitely a thing.

"I don't know what to say," I said softly.

"Where are you living now, since your apartment is no longer livable?"

"A loft in Dallas, do you need the address?" I asked, a bit confused. He nodded with his notepad out.

"I'll have some extra officers in the area, but until you tell me more, there's nothing else I can do." He said this as an invitation for me to keep speaking, but I didn't. Instead, I wrote down my new address, which I had to look up on Google Maps. We didn't say anything else, so I just left. I couldn't handle the sad, disappointed emotions filling the room. He cared, but it seemed too much for business partners. Maybe I reminded him of someone. Or he genuinely thought I was going to die. With so many victims, it made sense. But I didn't know for sure that the serial killer was after me.

And yet, when I saw Rin in the lobby, I felt safe. Nothing bad had happened to me so far. Even the shoot-up at the apartment didn't lead to a single scratch.

I was probably going to be fine. Probably.

By the time I got back to the loft, there was a package on the front step for me. The Church of Light was sending me gift baskets now. Baskets with wine and snacks, like from Father Abram's office. The gift basket came with a note promising everything I could ever want if I just quit being a necromancer. Yeah, because it was that easy.

"There were some poisoned ones mixed in, they've been disposed of," Rin said and scowled at me. "We should have thrown out the whole damn thing."

I looked at the basket in confusion. Why would someone waste perfectly good food? I started sifting through the assortment of crackers.

"You're keeping the snacks?" Rin asked disapprovingly from the kitchen. "Also, you got another note about the cat. Something about how your tongue will be next."

I sighed and put the basket on the counter and started rifling through it. I had almost forgotten about the chef I raised who had her tongue cut out. Gods, what kind of life was I living now?

"It's food, and you guys got rid of the poisoned ones," I countered.

"If a van comes up with free snacks, please don't get in."

I rolled my eyes, but I always wondered what would have happened if someone had offered as much when I was a kid. I really would have been snatched up. I stuffed coffee crackers in my mouth and dismissed the thought.

"By the way, do you know a guy named Jareth?" I asked. Rin didn't even flinch, but I could feel the tension growing in the air around me.

"He's a vampire. I don't know him personally," he said and pulled a bagel out of the toaster. I moved closer to him. He was quiet again like before when I mentioned wanting to train with the church. Rin was the worst omitter ever.

"What do you know?"

"Nothing I'd tell a danger magnet like you."

I wanted to be insulted, but he wasn't wrong. I really was surrounded by danger. It still didn't feel real. Rin got a call then. I watched his face as he answered but said nothing. As soon as he hung up, he turned to me, his expression serious.

"It looks like the gift basket came with an assassin," he said. I hesitantly put my crackers down but thought better of it and took a bite. "Does nothing phase you?" He asked with a laugh of disbelief.

I didn't know what he meant by that. I mean, the assassin didn't make it up here, and the food was fine. Plus, I had people protecting me. Why should I be scared? But I was scared. Inwardly, I knew it was only a matter of time before someone killed me. Would someone like Jennifer raise me from the dead? Would Malik question my zombie form? Would my killer get caught, or would it be a few more murders before any evidence came out?

My skin felt like ice, and yet I munched away and opened a Dr Pepper. As much as this all scared me, I still had stuff to do.

Maybe I should call Mrs. Bennett to let her know I was done thinking about her cat. I wasn't going to be able to find Aphrodite with everything else going on, and I didn't particularly like having so many death threats.

"Do you have any jobs tonight," Rin asked, pulling me from my thoughts.

"Nah, I figured I'd sleep early."

"So you can meet with Hale?"

I pressed the soda to my face to cool down my cheeks. Damn. I mean, yeah, but did he really have to say it so bluntly?

"Weren't you the one who said I should talk to him directly about staying here?" I countered, but it sounded like a child complaining, even to me.

"I did," he agreed. I sighed and set down the basket.

"You wear me out," I said and headed to the bedroom. It was just an excuse. He and I both knew it. I needed answers. I had to know when this conflict would end and whether the Church of Eternal Life was the issue he mentioned before or if they were a new threat.

I wasn't lying when I told Rin he made me tired, because within moments, I was out.

Hale had brought me to an abandoned movie theater. The seats were red, and the screen was stuck on a blue screen.

"You're still alive," Hale said from the top row. I was at the bottom. I quickly raced up the steps.

When I reached him, I could see the exhaustion on his face, bags under his eyes, and a solemn smile.

"Of course I'm alive," I said with a cheeky smile.

"What's wrong," he murmured and moved in closer, his face a hair's breadth away. My eyes widened in surprise. I was fine. There was nothing to talk about. But I could feel it, the anxiety and terror creeping below the surface.

"I keep getting death threats over a cat, and the two churches might want me dead," I said quickly. It wasn't a lie, and I needed to talk to him about this. As a statement, it wasn't nearly as vulnerable as I almost was. He didn't need to know my insecurities.

"The person I thought would target you hasn't made a move outside of gathering information on you," Hale said slowly, his eyes clouded as he seemed lost in thought. But then he looked at me, and there was a hint of amusement there. "But obviously, it was a good thing I sent Rin to help you. Otherwise, I wouldn't be able to see you again."

It sounded sweet until I realized he was implying I'd be dead in a ditch by now. Fair. I probably would be. But still.

"Is Jareth the one you were worried about?" I asked and watched as his jaw tightened.

"Yeah."

"Okay, so who is he?" I continued, confused about his reaction.

"He's another vampire. He was in South America for decades," Hale said and then looked into my eyes, his violet meeting my brown. "Lily, he likes to kill humans and vampires. He thinks everyone is a toy to entertain him. The peace we've fought so hard for? It bores him. He's here because I've been working with Congress on vampire rights, and since I'm one of the loudest vampire voices in politics, he wants me dead. But he can't just walk up to a Master Vampire and kill him, so he's looking for weaknesses."

"Why would I be a weakness?" I asked, and I knew I'd asked this before, but right now, he was looking at me and it felt more intimate.

"Well, for starters, I've spent quite a few nights in your dreams rather than at work," Hale pointed out in amusement. I blushed and looked away quickly. I mean, I supposed that was true.

When I couldn't help but look at him again, his eyes had an intensity I wasn't expecting, and there was a smile playing on his lips as though he was having fun being here with me. That was strange as hell given the situation. But, would it be wrong for me to be having fun too?

I realized then what I told Rin before. The loft. I had to find out how long I could stay and what I could do to make the stay a bit more permanent.

"I need a place to live," I blurted out with zero finesse whatsoever.

"But, you live in my loft," Hale said slowly. He stepped closer and tucked a loose strand of hair behind my ear. I nodded and swallowed hard. He smelled like lavender and lemongrass. It was intoxicating.

"Yeah, but only while you're protecting me."

"I could protect you forever."

I blinked in surprise. What? But his expression was serious as he looked at me, his gaze intense but full of something I didn't expect. Longing. Why would he want someone like me?

"Would you?" I asked, as though forever was really an option, but for a moment, I kind of wanted to pretend like this hot, powerful vampire had a thing for me. A real thing.

I shouldn't have asked. What if he said it was a joke? His piercing eyes took me in, flaws and all, and he smiled. It wasn't tiring, wasn't solemn, wasn't pitying. His smile had warmth to it. The kind the undead weren't supposed to have.

"Would you allow me to?" His counter was clever. How could I ask anything of someone already giving me protection, food, and a place to stay?

"Can I work with you to earn the loft?" I asked quickly. I didn't want to be indebted to him more than I already was. He leaned down and kissed me on the forehead.

"I'd rather you just accept my kindness. But I think that would hurt you more. How about you raise the dead for me on occasion." Technically, since I wasn't hired with Undead, Inc., as more than an intern, that meant I could do freelance work. I wasn't sure how legal this would wind up being given how dangerous his undead life seemed to be.

"What are we?"

"Two people who enjoy each other's company."

"Exclusively?" I asked.

"If you like."

I smiled at the vague response. "What are you going to do about Jareth?" He tensed then but kept hugging me.

"I'm going to kill him once I find him. He's been elusive but keeps sending me messages."

"The vampire and human deaths?"

"Yeah."

"Why isn't he coming after you directly?"

"Because he'd lose," Hale said simply, as if this were a fact. "Once I find him, it'll be over. Until then," he kissed my temple, "Stay alive."

With that, I woke up.

Chapter 17

Father Abram personally came to the loft to apologize for the attempted assassination via poisoned snacks.

"I hope you know it isn't the entire church that feels this way. Like with any organization, there are some zealots who feel the need to take away the choices of others," he said. He was wearing white robes and had bags under his reddened eyes. It looked like he'd been crying for hours.

"And you're not one of them?" Rin asked with a raised eyebrow. He was standing close to me, ready to move if needed. But Father Abram had been searched before he was allowed to enter.

"I can feel your anger and caution. I don't blame you. I don't mean Ms. Clarke any harm. She's a gifted girl," he said and gave me an exhausted smile. Gifted *poison*. "I'm truly sorry for all of this."

"I hope you know I'm not exactly in a rush to train my empath abilities anymore," I said. He nodded solemnly. "Maybe when I know your church won't try to kill me."

"I do understand. I hope you'll give me a chance in the future." He turned and left without waiting for a response. I was grateful for it. I was so tired of people trying to kill me. Too many at this point. But I also knew he wasn't going to give up on me that easily.

"You've got your work cut out for you," I said to Rin.

"It makes life interesting. It's not like you're doing anything to deserve it." Rin was casually leaning against the counter, his eyes intense as he looked me over, despite his nonchalant tone.

I wasn't so sure I didn't deserve it. So much death was connected to Hale and, by extension, me. Plus, the more involved I got, the more other people were noticing me too. I didn't realize the world was so dangerous.

Kind of ironic for a necromancer. I guess I was still a bit naive.

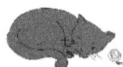

Thirty minutes later, we had pizza, and not long after the sun went down, I got a call from Malik.

"Hey, what's up?" I asked between bites of garden pizza.

"We have another double murder. I need you to meet me at the cafe across from your place," he said. I stopped breathing.

"It's that close?"

"Less than five minutes."

I hung up and shoved the pizza to the side.

"Another murder?" Rin set down his pepperoni and Canadian bacon.

"Yeah, and it's a bit too close for comfort."

I knew, I just knew this death was because of me. Rin wasn't allowed in, per usual, but he told me he'd be watching. The cafe's open sign was still glowing in the window despite the crime tape and the obscene amount of people at the crime scene. I couldn't get past the tape at first until Detective Malik saw me at the edge and motioned the officers to let me through.

I walked into the cafe. It was so different from when Rin and I came here together. The paintings on the wall were done by kids in the neighborhood according to the markers. The shop, with its circular tables and velvet couches, still smelled of coffee and stale pastries. I was counting the cake pops in the case when Detective Malik shoved a chicken into my hands. This made me look at the one thing I could've gone without seeing.

Two girls, one a vampire[36] who looked to be early twenties and the other a teenager,[37] were lying in a bloody puddle on the floor. The two were shot repeatedly until their limbs looked like they'd break apart if I touched them. I gasped and pulled out my blade. Within seconds, the animal's blood was trickling down my hands, and before I realized what I was doing, I was raising the teenager from the dead. The process pulled her skin together, healing her for the moment, as her eyes began to focus.

I just couldn't look at their bodies anymore. Bullet wounds. It had to be silver bullets to kill a vampire, but really, silver bullets could kill just about anything. This included young shop girls.

I was so quick that it wasn't until after the zombie was moving toward me that Jennifer arrived. If looks could kill, I would be six feet under with an obituary already. I forgot my zombie's dead coworker. That is, until my zombie was screaming bloody murder and clinging to my legs.

---

[36] Cassidy Samson (she/her)
[37] Jamie Calloway (she/her)

"Cover the body," Detective Malik ordered, but it was too late. The zombie was sobbing dry tears as she clutched me so tightly, I knew I'd bruise. I fucked up. I couldn't believe I instinctually raised her without waiting for Malik to give the go-ahead.

"Control it," Jennifer hissed, already beside me looking down at my zombie. It?! She was a person. Sure, she died, but that didn't make her a thing. That thought alone brought me back.

"What's your name?" I asked and knelt beside her. As I moved, she moved too. Me acknowledging her seemed to have calmed her down. I felt like I could soothe her pain and help her forget what happened. I cringed. Was I really considering taking away her free will? This grief was hers. Who was I to force her to be okay?

"Jamie Calloway," she whispered. Malik stepped forward then.

"I need to know what happened here," he said and kneeled as well. He was so close, my skin became clammy as I scooted a few inches away.

"He was mad, a vampire. He walked in and threw things, chairs, stuff like that. We were closing, so no one else was here. He wanted to kill her. She begged. She's a scaredy cat, always running away. Spiders especially. I stood in front of her and said no, but he didn't listen. I don't know why. And then it hurt. Everything hurt. I was bleeding, and I saw him kill her. She didn't want to die. Me too, but... but," her words were broken. Her eyes clouded again.

"What did he look like?" Malik demanded and grabbed her shoulders. But she was just shaking her head repeatedly.

"She's breaking," I told him and could feel her sanity slipping away. Gods, she had to be like fifteen. The vampire girl didn't look much older, and she was newly changed too. For a moment, it was like I was at the graveyard again for that test, trying to age a vampire. I still didn't understand it, but just being near her, I could tell. I realized then that I'd never managed to "age" Hale before. I noticed it with the other two, but with him, it didn't automatically come up. But looking at this dead child, I wiped the tears from my eyes.

"What happens if she breaks?" He asked and released his grip.

"Then she becomes useless, a *corpse* and not a reanimated person," Jennifer answered before I could. Malik stepped away; I could feel his defeat. This case must be hard on him. My hands seemed so small, powerless, and yet, I wanted to use them like I did on Sebastian. This time though, I wanted it to be different.

I cupped Jamie's face in my hands and willed her to feel safe. I wanted her to trust me and to realize she was no longer in danger. We wanted to help, and if she cooperated, we could find the killer. Her eyes were so big and round, but instead of sadness, they were full of hope. "You'll do it? You'll help us?" she asked and clutched my hands.

"I need your help first," I countered with a small smile. She returned it and turned to Detective Malik.

"Can you repeat your question?" she asked. Jennifer's eyes were glued to Jamie, but she didn't look as relieved as Malik did. Instead, her lips were pressed tightly together, and she crossed her arms over her chest. This woman could never be pleased.

"He was tall with black hair and tattoos covering his face and arms. They were like black squiggles. His eyes were black too, and his skin was super tan. Like, almost brown," Jamie said, her voice quickening as she adapted to her reanimation. A glow of warm pride filled my chest as I watched her become the teenage girl she should have been.

"Did he say a name or tell you what he wanted?" Malik asked. I tried to give him some space as Malik moved closer to Jamie, trying to distract her from the covered corpse by us.

"I need you here in case she starts to break again," he breathed in my ear. I nodded, but felt a slight tingling of nervousness coming from Malik. Why was he nervous? He's interacted with a few zombies around me at this point.

Her puppy face caught me off guard. Apparently, me attempting to leave hurt Jamie's feelings.

"I didn't get a name. I just know he wanted to kill a girl named Lily Clarke, but he couldn't get her. So, he came here instead," she said making me freeze. Everyone was looking at me. Well shit.

Chapter 18

I'd been in the interrogation room for three hours. Rin wasn't there. Of course he wouldn't get caught by the cops. The zombie wasn't there either. Just me. Just me because I had a teenage zombie who liked to talk about angry vampires that wanted to kill a defenseless necromancer. Detective Malik came in with a cup of coffee for me. He had the cup in one hand and several sugars and creams in the other. Good cop, maybe?

I smiled and immediately turned the rich black coffee into a sweetness that was almost as light as me. "You prefer cream with a splash of coffee," he said in disgust. He seemed to catch himself then and flashed me a smile that almost looked sincere.

"I like sugar," I said and took a giant swig of my drink. Okay, so yeah, this was a lot of sugar. A ton. Too much. Good Gods, this was awful. But I forced myself to finish it off with another gulp and tried to pretend like I didn't just drink liquid sludge.

"Are you ready to talk to me?" he asked and folded his hands under his chin. My throat dried as I tried to think of some kind of answer. But what was I supposed to say? I'm being hunted down by a group of extremist vampires because I may or may not be dating a hot guy named Hale. I mean, no one told me not to tell. It felt stupid because I never even thought to talk to him about this. I guess it just didn't feel real. Like, maybe someone would jump out and say "Just kidding! Who would want to kill you? And hot vampires? So not in your league."

But this was real.

People wanted me dead, and other people died in the process. Hale told me Jareth might be after me. I was just so busy thinking about the cat and the churches that I really assumed Jareth wasn't that big of a deal. But if that killer was the one Rin was protecting me from- I felt so nauseous.

It wasn't until the girls at the cafe died that I realized anyone else could die if these crazy people couldn't reach me. It was horrifying and made me feel all the guilt and worthlessness. Was my life really more important than two baristas? Why did anyone have to die? But maybe I was naive. And maybe there was a worse killer out there than the cat stealer and the churches.

"What do you want to talk about?" I asked and looked at him with the biggest eyes I could muster. He didn't seem impressed. I needed to stall for time until I could think this through.

"I want to talk about why your zombie said that you were a target of the same person we've been investigating for the other human and vampire murders," he said and leaned forward. I scooted back and tried to look away, but the intensity of his eyes made it hard to avoid him.

"Zombies say the craziest things," I said with a forced smile. His stare intensified. Damn. I guess witty retorts wouldn't save me today. "Okay, so yeah, I have a bodyguard because I was told someone might be after me. I don't really know more than that," I said quickly and stumbled over the words. It was probably a mistake, but it was an uncorrected mistake. Malik's hands dropped as he crossed his arms.

"Who told you you were in danger? How did they know?"

I sighed. I told him all I knew. Minus Sebastian, because holy hell, I wasn't touching that with a ten-foot pole. But I did tell Malik about the Church of Light, as well as the cat notes. Plus, I let him know I had a feeling the gunmen at my apartment were because of the cat, but I didn't have any proof on that one.

When I was done, he didn't seem happy.

"I asked you three times now why you had a bodyguard, and every time your answer has been different. Why didn't you come to me?"

He seemed to realize how odd that sounded and clarified. "I meant the police. You knew this was being investigated. I could charge you with obstruction of justice."

I laid my head on the table. Fuuuck. I was totally getting arrested. He sighed.

"We're going to put you in a safe house with police protection. No one will get to you. We will find whoever is after you, Lily. You'll be safe," Detective Malik assured me in the most unassuring way possible.

I mean, if the police were going to take care of me, maybe a vacation was in order. I could just relax and not take any more jobs—oh my Gods. Mrs. Bennett! "I need to make a phone call," I said much louder than I meant to. Malik frowned but then motioned for me to follow him. "I promise, this is important! If I tell Mrs. Bennett that I'm off the cat case, then that'll be one less group of people trying to kill me."

The phone was an old landline, but I'd used these before. At this point, I had her number memorized. I didn't even remember my mom's number. An unfamiliar voice answered the phone, which is about what I expected. "This is Lily Clarke, Mrs. Bennett's necromancer she hired to help find Aphrodite. I wanted to talk to her about the arrangement," I said, trying to keep my voice cool.

"Very well, I will see if she is available," her butler or someone equally bougie said and left me on hold. It was about ten seconds before Mrs. Bennett's frantic voice filled my ear.

"You found her? You found my baby!" she screamed. I wet my lips and tried to think how to phrase this. There's no way I'd get another opportunity to call her anytime soon.

"No, but I want to go ahead and get off the case. I keep getting death threats," I said quickly. Money would be amazing right now. The kind of money she offered, especially. Enough to run away to another country maybe. France. I liked the idea of France. But I was sick of my life being threatened.

"Our last agreement was $8,000. I'm going to make it $16,000. I'll tell my boyfriend to stop hunting you or he'll have to foot your bill," she spat and hung up the phone before I could respond. Well shit, looked like I was still on the case. Right when I was about to get put into protective custody too, since that would obviously help me find the stupid cat. And what the hell did she mean her *boyfriend* was hunting me?!

"You're actually still tracking her cat?" Malik asked. His tall frame leaned against the hallway wall as he stared at me. He frowned at me. "Didn't you say you've been getting death threats because of it?" He paused then and tilted his head. "She said she would tell her boyfriend to stop hunting you."

172

"One day, I will develop life preservation skills, but yeah, her boyfriend might be after me. I guess, no one bothered to tell me that until today," I informed Malik, my expression a mask of remorse. However, the idea of $16,000 definitely made me a little less remorseful. Now I just needed to not die and somehow simultaneously find a cat while in a safe house.

Malik sighed, like a disappointed parent.

After a moment, he looked at me. "There is someone here to see you. A priest," he said and motioned for me to follow him.

"I'm supposed to be under protective custody. Am I allowed to see anyone?" I asked feeling grumpy. The last thing I wanted was to talk to Father Abram. At least it was highly unlikely this was a priest from the Church of Eternal Life. It was too early in the day for a vampire priest to visit.

"It's up to you. You're always allowed to see religious figures," Malik said plainly.

I was led to a private room where Father Abram sat at a lone metal table with dim lighting. Detective Malik leaned against the wall while I sat across from the priest.

"You seem to have gotten yourself into some trouble since I last saw you."

"Yeah, people still want me dead," I shrugged. It was a bit callous, but what was I supposed to say in this situation?

"I'm sorry," he said. "At least the church hasn't done anything since the gift incident." He smiled sheepishly as though this was embarrassing rather than life-threatening.

Malik was facing away, but I knew better than to think he wasn't listening. Probably more intensely than I was.

"How are you so sure?" I asked with narrowed eyes.

He pressed his lips tightly together. "I guess you're right. I wish I could tell you that the Church won't go after you again. Although I'm of a high rank, I'm not the leader. I can't use authority over others in my same position or their loyalists."

"We're going to need to discuss this," Malik said with narrowed eyes, finally joining the conversation. He didn't look at me, but at this point, he was told about one person and an organization that wanted me dead. Looks like there'd be a whole different police investigation happening soon.

"What's the plan then? Why are you here?"

"I'm able to send some people to protect you. There's a powerful witch[38] that can help. She's stronger than you might think. She's an employee at a witchcraft store called Bewitched Denton." It seemed silly for a priest to be working with a witch, but I guess they weren't considered heathens like me.

"She will be under police protection," Malik said, breaking his silence. The priest looked at him for the first time and nodded.

"I'm sure your officers are capable; I would just like to offer additional assistance."

"After this investigation is done, then you two can discuss this more," Malik said and looked at me.

---

[38] Cassia (she/her)

"I've taken up too much of your time," Father Abram said and stood up. I gave him a thin smile and watched him go. Maybe a witch would be helpful. But it looked like Malik wasn't up for trusting anyone. My eyes widened then.

"Wait, I can bring Rin, right? My current bodyguard?" I asked quickly, becoming a bit flustered. Malik's expression was firm. Was I really going somewhere without Rin? Apparently, the answer was yes.

Chapter 19

I was put in a small house in Mineral Wells. It was a smallish town, at least way smaller than Dallas anyway. Two officers were assigned to me, a guy named Bob[39] and a girl named Debra[40]. They seemed nice enough and stuffed the fridge with frozen food.

"Any idea when I'll be able to go home?" I asked and grabbed a spaghetti one to munch on.

"Want Texas garlic bread to go with it?" Bob asked with a giant smile.

"We don't know, hon," Debra answered me and rolled her eyes at Bob. "But we'll let you know as soon as we know something." I didn't know what expression I had, but she gave me a sympathetic smile. "Detective Malik is good at what he does. Young, sure, but so smart. He'll get this case solved soon, and you'll be able to go back to your life."

I smiled at her. She felt so kind and homey. I wanted to believe her.

"What do you do for work, Lily?" Bob asked as he set a timer on the oven.

"I'm a necromancer."

"Oh, so dead people. We deal with dead people too," he said with a laugh. Debra smacked him playfully.

"Stupid joke. How about something fun? What do you like to do?"

---

[39] Officer Bob Trells (he/him)
[40] Officer Debra Franky (she/her)

It was such an unexpected question. I didn't know what to say until the microwave dinged. "I like eating." They both laughed. When food finished cooking, we sat down and ate together. Bob wound up making the bread. They were like hokey parents, the kind I wished I had growing up.

Debra slept in the same room as me while Bob took a spot on the couch. There was a good chance I'd have to be here for a week or even a month. I missed Rin though, and my cat. I knew he'd take care of her though. I hoped someone would tell Amy and Jazz I was okay. I didn't want them to think I was dead or something. Even if I could be before the end of this.

While I lay in bed, I pulled out my phone and saw a text from Rin. I didn't realize he had my number.

Rin: How are you doing?

Me: Fine, I actually ate food.

Rin: Healthy or carb-y?

Me: Carbs. Duh.

Rin: Better than iced coffee for every meal.

Me: LOL

Rin: I'm nearby.

Me: I thought you might be. I miss you.

Rin: Yeah, it's been fun. But it looks like it'll be over soon.

Me: I'm glad. G'nite.

Rin: Sleep well.

In my dream, I was sitting at a park bench under an impossible amount of stars. I couldn't pick out constellations in general, but in general, it seemed like there were way too many up there. It's part of how I knew it was a dream. And if it was a dream then-

"Lily," Hale said and leaned against the bench. I thought he'd sit beside me at least, but he was looking up at the sky.

"Do you choose these settings?" I asked him, making him smile softly, but he didn't look at me.

"They're all tied to important memories," Hale said, and his voice sounded far off. It felt like he was stalling.

I kicked my feet idly under the table and looked up at the sky. My hands gripped the edge of the bench as I enjoyed the night air. Real or not, it was nice.

"I couldn't pay them to let Rin come along, so he's in a nearby cabin," Hale said finally, making me glance over at him.

"You tried to pay off the police?" I asked, stunned. Wasn't that illegal? And, like, probably expensive?

"It didn't work," Hale pointed out with an amused smile at my reaction.

"Okay, but you still tried."

He sighed and pushed his blond hair back with his fingers. "I did, because you're in danger and my best assassin is stuck on the sidelines."

Did he mean to tell me Rin was an assassin? Because I sure as *hell* didn't know that.

"I take it you haven't found Jareth?" I asked hesitantly and pulled my knees up to my chest. It felt a bit colder now.

Hale didn't say anything, which was as much an answer as anything else. He looked at me then, his violet eyes darker than usual.

"Don't die," he said firmly, and I woke up.

I heard gunshots. What was happening?! Debra had me hide under the bed. Weren't the police supposed to be keeping me hidden? Her gun was drawn as she made her way to the living room. I could hear the front door get kicked open.

"Where's the necromancer?!"

The voice sounded monstrous. Full of rage. The hate was so vivid it was like slime crawling over my skin. Hot and sticky.

"It's just me and my husband. Get the fuck out," Debra yelled. Shots fired again. I could hear someone dying. A cry. Squelch. And if I wanted to, I could raise them from the dead. I felt sick to my stomach.

"Why is the Church here? Since when does the Church of Light try to kill people?!" Bob demanded, making me stifle a cry of relief. Thank Gods, he was still alive. But the Church?! Poisoned snacks were one thing, but holy shit guys.

"Find the girl," the first voice shouted as gunshots continued. "Vampire! There's a vampi-"

"Move." Whoever's voice this was commanded power. Absolute silence followed. Were they dead? The newcomer was different, much more intense, and definitely here for me. Fuck.

The door to my bedroom opened. Two steps and then the bed I was hiding under was thrown off me.

"Plan's changed. He wants you alive," a tall man covered in black tattoos said.

"You're the one. The one killing all the humans and vamps," I breathed out. He smiled, and it was the most sickening thing I've ever seen. It was a stark and horrible contrast to Bob's dad joke smile.

"And you're the one Jareth wants."

Everything went black.

Chapter 20

"I'm so sorry," Hale said as he held me in his arms. We were lying in his bed with sunlight streaming in through the curtains.

"Isn't light dangerous for you?" I asked, not fully understanding him. Why was he apologizing? But it was so warm. I felt safe there.

"Not while you're here. In dreams with you, sunlight is allowed," he whispered. "Lily, do you remember what happened?"

"What do you mean?"

"You've been kidnapped. Jareth has you now. I thought he was going to kill you, but instead, you've been captured alive."

I tried to think about the words coming out of his mouth. It just seemed so ridiculous. Why would anyone want me? Kidnapping seemed like something that only happened in the movies.

"I guess that's life."

My callousness made him squeeze me tight.

"I'm so sorry," he said. The words sounded hollow though, like his mind was somewhere else. "The Church of Light sent some gunmen to kill you at the safehouse. But then Jareth's right-hand man showed up, and that's what made us unable to intervene. If it was just humans, it would have been easy to get you out. I'm going to track you down and save you. Then, we'll go on that date." It still didn't feel real. None of it. I was going to wake up to Rin lecturing me on food, and I'd have to keep looking for the dumb cat. There's no way I was really...

"I'll find you," he breathed against me.

I woke up.

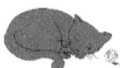

I was in a room with a twin-sized bed, two dressers, and a chair with a desk. It was much more normal than the one I had in Hale's loft. I ran to the door and tried to open it. Of course, it was locked. There was a thing called *being kidnapped*. That meant I couldn't escape.

So, it looked like Hale wasn't lying when he said I'd been captured. I tried to remember what happened. The police station. Yeah. I called Mrs. Bennett. Malik said something about custody. I remembered two nice officers feeding me, and Rin texted. And then... oh Gods. They died. I think they died.

I went over to the desk and started searching drawers. Nothing that could pick locks. Not that I knew how to do that, but you know, maybe I could figure it out. There were a ton of poetry and fantasy books. Guess I wouldn't get too bored while I was here. I walked around the room. No windows, the vents were tiny, and only one door. There was absolutely nothing I could do to get out. The vents were too skinny for my ass, and they were on the ceiling. The idea of John Wick-ing my way out of here seemed slim to none.

I opened a fantasy about dragons and demons. I guess I could read to pass the time. I tried to play it cool, but my stomach was in knots. Just fake it till you make it. Don't let them think they got to you. And maybe, just maybe, shove it all down like you always do. I got about halfway through the book when the door opened. The tall, tattooed vampire stood in the doorway. His eyes were so dark, they were almost black as he stared at me.

"Who are you?" I asked. If I made it out of here alive, I could give the info to Malik.

"That's not what you should be worrying about right now," he said and walked slowly into the room. I quickly moved to the other side of the bed, as far from him as I could get. Sure, vampires had super speed, but at least I felt safe for the moment.

"At least I'm not dead," I said with a smile, making him laugh harshly.

"You're only alive because you're wanted by so many organizations. We lucked out that we had the police station tapped. To think, we could have bypassed the wards by paying attention to a damn *cat* case you had."

"Oh." Stupid goddamn cat haters.

"My Master is ready to see you now. Are you coming, or am I forcing you?" he asked in a patient voice. It sounded dangerous. Although he didn't feel angry, I could sense something dark and dangerous about him. The fact that he was a known serial killer probably added to that feeling.

I walked slowly toward him, and he turned to lead the way. I got to see his tattoos for the first time and realized they were words. I couldn't tell what language, but the squiggles of foreign letters wrapped around him like vines. The building was a maze of hallways with no rooms. There were so many cameras, they felt redundant, but given that Hale was trying to track them down, I guess the security made sense.

Ironically, I was probably safer here than anywhere else I'd been so far. Rin came to mind. He'd probably be pissed if I said that to his face. I hoped he wasn't too worried. Then again, I was going to die here at some point. There's no way I wouldn't. But if I could keep Jareth curious about me, maybe I could live a bit longer. I caressed the indent of the totem in my pants pocket. I had at least one trick up my sleeve. Or down my pants, I guess. I didn't even know how to use the damn thing, really. But- I guess I could stab someone with it? I thought about how it sucked up my blood before and shivered.

We walked through a set of double doors and wound up in a dining hall. The table was meant for twelve and was full of food with a single empty plate. There was a glass of red wine on the table, which was meh. I immediately sat down and began piling food on. Mashed potatoes, rare-cooked meat, and a variety of steamed vegetables. It was the best meal I'd had in ages.

I took a particularly large bite of steak just as a voice laughed from next to me. I nearly choked. A man was sitting there with white-blond hair that was shoulder-length and poofy, long fingers that were crossed under his chin, and a thin yet abnormally beautiful face. I swallowed hard and took a sip of some wine. I preferred Dr Pepper, but kidnapping victims shouldn't demand their favorite drinks.

I winced at the flavor. It tasted like cough medicine.

"For someone in such a precarious situation, you don't seem concerned that the food is poisoned." He sounded like he could be a singer. Every word was melodic.

"I figured you would have killed me by now. Poisoning food just seems wasteful," I shrugged.

"Hence why I poisoned the wine."

I choked again and wound up coughing so hard that tears streamed down my eyes. The vampire laughed, and it was just as pretty as before.

"I'm joking," he said with a wide smile. "I have no interest in killing you while so many others want you dead. It'd be a bit boring to help the people I hate." He said it with such matter-of-factness that I found myself believing him.

"It's just both churches right, no one else?" I asked hesitantly. I mean, two sects of people wanting to kill me was still pretty bad, but I wanted to at least confirm it wasn't worse than I thought.

"Yes, but not the entirety of either church," he said with a shrug. His eyes glittered. "We always assume we know how dangerous something is based on its *potential*. But what if we don't truly know the potential of the dangerous thing?"

Great. Riddles. I turned back to my mashed potatoes. Garlic parmesan. The greatest accomplishment of mankind. "I'd like to understand your potential before I kill you."

Well, there you go. Even with his ego on the line, he still wanted to kill me at some point. It was getting boring.

"You just want me dead because you think Hale cares about me, right?" I asked as I held out a spoonful of garlic mashed potatoes threateningly. Garlic hurts vampires, right? Jareth looked down at my spoon in amusement and waved it away, purposely letting his hand graze it.

His gaze measured me, and his lips pursed. But then he was smiling all over again. "I know you two aren't lovers, if that's what you mean."

"So why do you want me dead so badly? Seemed like you had your henchman go through quite a few people to get to me," I said in between bites. "Hey, you got a soda instead? Wine is fancy and all, but it's not my taste." He looked behind me at the doorway, and within moments, a woman was beside me with four different soda options. Dr Pepper. It's all I needed when in a life-or-death situation.

"It was cute seeing a fellow Master Vampire try to protect a human. I wanted to see his resolve. But then you became too interesting. Not your fault really. There's just a potential about you that causes fear in the undead."

I didn't like the way that sounded. My hands were shaking to the point where I couldn't hold my fork. It seemed like the adrenaline was gone.

"I don't know if you know this, but you have a taste," he said, leaning in close. Unlike Hale, this wasn't sexy at all. Instead, it felt dangerous. Like one wrong move, and he'd bite my face off. "You make the undead like you and want to protect you." His words sounded gentle, but he was gripping my arm so tight, I would have screamed if it wouldn't have taken the air out of me. "A human with so much power over the dead, almost as much power as I hold over my vampires," he whispered.

I remembered then how all my human zombies cared about me. They were protective and seemed so real. Was it because I was an empath? Tears streamed down my cheeks. I wasn't sure if it was from the pain of my arm being bruised or if it was the realization that I was truly a monster. Either way, I couldn't get the tears to stop. Jareth smiled at me with the teeth of a predator.

"Yes, truly dangerous. You'll be living here with me for the time being," he said and released me. I gasped for breath, and that movement sent a shooting pain up my arm. He left me alone with a soda I no longer wanted. After what seemed like an hour, the serial killer vampire led me back to the room I was in before. I had no interest in reading or anything else. The bed called me, and so I slept.

Maybe I could at least have some good dreams.

Chapter 21

Hale didn't join me in my dreams. Even so, when I woke up, I wasn't alone.

I was given a human servant[41]. Seemed like a gross descriptor for a girl who took care of my meals, clothing, and entertainment. But that's how the vampires described her. She had a multitude of bites on her skin, mostly scarred, and a faraway gaze. She wouldn't tell me her name. She just kept saying she was there to serve.

This made me think she was a thrall.

"I've brought you iced coffee," she said from the doorway. I was sitting at the desk reading yet another book. The fantasies weren't bad. If anything, I was surprised someone like Jareth would have this kind of taste in literature. It'd been about ten meals since I'd been there. So maybe three or four days. Wasn't quite sure. Without any windows, I was just winging it when it came to time.

"I'm running out of books," I sighed. She gave a smile then, something I hadn't seen from her until now.

"If you like those books, then I can get you more."

"Are these yours?"

"Yes. You're staying in my room."

Well, that was news to me. I looked around at the bare bedroom and took in a new appreciation of it. This girl lived here, although she wasn't staying here now. But this was her home. Or maybe it wasn't. She could have been kidnapped like me. I couldn't imagine anyone willing to live with these psychopaths. She could have been a thrall,

---

[41] Human servant (she/her)

but that didn't mean she was brought here willingly. If that were the case, then she'd never be able to leave, and if the vampire who thralled her died, then so would she. Gods, that was depressing.

"No need to change anything you're doing. This room will come back to me soon."

The way she said that implied she knew something about my situation. "So, does that mean I'm moving?"

"Well, you're going to receive some training to see if you can work for Jareth. If you can't, then I assume he'll kill you." She went from not saying much to saying the most terrifying things.

I opened my mouth to ask more, but she just forced the iced coffee on me and stepped to the side. The serial killer was in the doorway. I learned his name was Barry. It seemed a bit anticlimactic given the brutality of the murders he committed, but I guess not everyone got a cool name.

"We have a necromancer[42] here to see you," he said and showed way too many teeth as he motioned for a man to come inside. He was old with a worn face and calloused hands. He was wearing a paper-thin large grey shirt and baggy pants that looked like they'd never been washed. I glanced at the girl, but she was already leaving the room. Soon it was just me and the old man. He smelled like graveyard dirt, an old and musty smell that had a hint of magic to it.

"No point in names." He smiled at me grimly, then held out his hand. "May I see your totem?" The question took me off

---

[42] Master Necromancer (he/him)

guard. I'd kept it in my pocket this whole time. It felt comforting to have it. I handed it to him and was immediately backhanded so hard I fell to the floor and spat blood. "Never give away your essence. A totem is a piece of your very soul."

I could barely catch the words through the ringing in my ears. I'd never been hit like that before. My cheek hurt so freaking bad. He held his hand out to me; even with his aggression, I didn't hesitate to take it. But touching him disgusted me, and I quickly withdrew my hand once I was on my feet. Despite his sudden act of violence, I could feel his genuine fear as he looked at me. I couldn't be the one scaring him, so it must have been Jareth. What did he threaten this old man with?

"You have no prior training?"

"Sorry, I've mostly been self-taught. My job doesn't train necromancers." I held my cheek with my hand; it was already swelling. And lifting my arm made me wince from Jareth's aggression. Everyone here was beating me up.

"That's good. It means I won't have to fight any bad habits. Most necromancers have no idea what they're doing," he said and flashed a grin. His teeth were grey and decaying. I pressed my lips tightly together so I couldn't show my disgust.

"What does Jareth want with me?"

"That, I know nothing. The dead? I know a lot. Let's stick with my strengths, shall we?" He spread his legs and held out his arms. I noticed a totem in his hand, which he used to slice down his arm, oozing out black blood. His totem was dark, almost like night. There were quite a few bones, no plants that I could see, and several strands of hair of

193

varying colors, like he tore them from different heads. A shiver ran down my spine. Why was he doing this here? It's not like this was a gravesite, there shouldn't be corpses around. I could hear feet shuffle down the hall, and then around a dozen zombies entered the room. They stood along the walls and stared blankly ahead. It was like an undead army just waiting for the command to strike.

"I don't understand," I said slowly. They were falling apart, some were missing half their faces, and yet, I knew they were newly raised. How did he do it?

"You still use blood and have to see the body, don't you?" he asked, his tone snarky. I felt my face redden. He acted like it was a bad thing. That's the only way I knew how to do it, and it worked. So of course I'd stick with it. "It's fine. I can work with you. Some of my apprentices couldn't even raise the dead when I started with them. Had to rush them through the trials to become a necromancer and everything."

"What are you going to teach me?"

"Everything."

Somehow, we had permission to be in the corpse disposal room. This must have been where those zombies of his came from. It was only a few doors down from the room I'd been trapped in. The necromancer told me it was the most secret place in the building. I doubted that. It smelled like shit, vomit, and sweetbreads. I plugged my nose, but the old man slapped my hand away.

"Breathe it all in, girl," he said. I closed my eyes and winced as the smell made its way inside my mouth. My stomach felt hot and thick as I tried not to gag. I opened my eyes as he dragged a corpse on the floor over to me. "Know this one?" he asked, forcing the half-decomposed face towards me. I shook my head.

I couldn't even tell the sex. Their skin was bloated and had a reddish-yellow tinge. Everywhere I looked, there were bodies in various stages of decay. The smell was so overpowering, I could taste it. The hair was gone, and maggots were crawling all over. That alone was enough to make me gag. I choked on the air and coughed so hard I threw up bile on the ground, just barely missing the body and the old man.

"That's good then, no connection, and now you have to raise it from the dead," he said.

"I need to bleed an animal somehow."

"Lies! Lies told by amateurs. The totem is enough. Cut yourself with the totem and it'll raise the dead alone. You might as well own another thing in this world, right?"

I forced myself to swallow the hot saliva that was building up in my mouth. I didn't want to touch this person. At this point, they looked more like a science experiment. A body so bloated, it looked like it'd pop.

"Now, do it. Raise it."

Easier said than done. I wiped my clammy palms on my sweats and stared down at the empty holes for eyes. If they were dead down here, then they were probably tortured. Someone hurt them badly enough for them to die. Did I really want to raise someone like that? Could I really bring them right back where they had died? It was cruel.

"How can I?" I asked as he thrust the body toward me. Maggots splashed onto the ground in a sickening *plup* sound.

"Figure it out."

Great. I inhaled and this time managed not to throw up, even as I watched the maggots squirm on top of the body. A coldness washed over me so strongly that the nausea left. I could do this. My power wanted to. My ability thrummed against my skin, a cold breeze.

I closed my eyes and reached out my hand, careful not to touch the corpse directly.

I could feel the breath of something else reaching back. I focused on that energy and began to tug with the coldness within me. My totem shook in my hand, and without hesitation, I pulled out my totem and used the mausoleum shard from my to slash my palm. It felt like water, icy water reaching out. When I opened my eyes, a young man was kneeling naked in front of me and my hand was already healing. My totem seemed to be *drinking* my blood. Just like the day I made it. So freaking gross.

"Why am I back?" he asked, his terrified brown eyes staring into mine like I had the answers.

"Your zombie looks whole. That's more than I expected," the old man said and patted the zombie on the shoulder. The zombie flinched and crawled towards me. "Ah, you've got the touch." The old man gave me a sinister smile, then grabbed my zombie by the nape of the neck. Within moments, he was rotting.

"No," I screamed and reached out with my powers. My zombie made a noise so loud and horrific it deafened me as I concentrated with all my will. It was no use; he was decomposing again. I could feel his pain, horror, and confusion as he screamed. He was being forced to decompose while still conscious. I couldn't save him.

Tears streamed down my face as I reached out and held him in my arms. His smoky scent was turning back into sweetbread. I could feel the maggots crawling on my skin, and I didn't care. He was mine, and he was dying.

"Your sympathy for the dead is charming."

I didn't feel so charming right now. Rage built up inside me as I held the corpse in my arms. I released him and hated myself for waiting so long. Had I done it earlier, when the decomposition started, then he wouldn't have had to go through that pain. Could zombies feel pain? It was my first time seeing it. Whatever the old man did, it was evil and transcended death.

"Why did you do that?" My voice didn't sound like me. It was gargled and full of monstrous loathing. I wanted to kill him. I needed him to feel what my zombie felt as he died in my arms.

"You're so cute. This naivety will hold you back. I can make you stronger, girl. Don't throw away this opportunity."

I couldn't focus on the words anymore. The bugs crawling on my flesh meant nothing either. Instead, I was glaring at him. When I hurt Sebastian, it was out of fear. Right now? This was rage.

He could help me become a better necromancer, maybe. But I could kill him without raising a finger. I used every ounce of my loathing and directed it at him. His smile was gone in an instant, and I was bathing in blood.

Chapter 22

I woke up in the room again. The servant girl sat next to me and was reading a book to herself. As soon as she saw my open eyes, she shot up out of her seat and ran to the door. There was fear. She never seemed scared of me before.

Within moments, Barry stood in the doorway. He had a smirk on his face. "You're a firecracker. I didn't expect that," he said.

I frowned.

"What are you talking about?"

"You don't remember nearly killing our necromancer? You did such a wonderful job. We had to kidnap a priest to keep him alive."

I couldn't understand. What on earth was he talking about? It hit me then. The room with the dead bodies. Maggots. My poor zombie. He was so scared. I had hurt the old man. I couldn't fully remember what I'd done, but I did it on purpose. I didn't feel guilty though. If anything, it felt justified. Fuck him. He hurt something that meant him no harm and was defenseless. I never wanted to witness something that terrible ever again.

"Well, no matter. Turns out you've got another ability we didn't expect. I guess you don't want to die."

"What do you mean?"

"Jareth keeps all the interesting things alive, as long as you keep him entertained." His words sounded like a threat. They probably were. I was in a hostage situation after all.

"So, I need to keep trying to kill his people to stay alive," I said dryly. Barry laughed, and it was such a gross sound.

"Killing people always keeps people alive," Barry said and flashed his fangs at me. My mind flashed to all the people he killed before, and whatever expression I made caused him to smile wider. "You'd be surprised. Back when vampires were hunted down, we cared more about our kind. It was *special* to be turned into one of us, and if you survived the hunters? You were beyond the label of special and became *extraordinary*. After all, humans wanted us dead, and you were above them. Humans are the prequel to the ultimate state of being. To associate with them is to associate with animals. They're beneath us."

The way he spoke to me about this was as though I was one of them, and it made my mouth dry. I stayed quiet until he finally smirked and left the room.

My next meal was with Jareth. He had the servant girl on his lap, while I had a variety of pasta and bread. I guess he was fattening me up to eat me later. I hated the way she looked at him like he was her world. It just made me see even more that she was thralled and could never truly escape.

"Barry told you how much I loved your work, didn't he?"

I ignored him and instead inhaled the shrimp alfredo. It was real shrimp. Like, I was eating actual seafood, not imitation. He could fuck off for all I cared.

"Is that ability why the church wants you so bad? Can't say I blame them. It's a beautiful talent."

I choked.

I had been avoiding thinking about it, but there was so much blood. I almost murdered him. It was way worse than Sebastian, because at least Sebastian was an accident. I was becoming a monster. He leaned forward; His highlighter blue blazer and bright yellow undershirt were blinding. He looked like he came out of a roller rink's carpet. It distracted me from the thick smell of blood I was so happily reminiscing about. I really was turning into a monster.

Blood dripped down the servant girl's neck and onto her shoulder. I watched her dull eyes and hoped wherever she was, it wasn't here.

"You look so scared," he said as the girl slipped from his grasp to step out of his way. She still didn't look present. Hopefully she was in a safer place once she got out of her trance. He didn't even acknowledge her. Instead, he was fully focused on me. His eyes were a swirl of green and blue. They felt like they had some kind of magic. He reeked of danger.

"Humans are frail little things, aren't they," Jareth said in amusement. "They think they're so powerful, but in one touch or one glance, they can become ensnared. Completely trapped within our power. It's cute that vampires are trying to act like equals and even protectors when we've always been better."

I glanced away; this was similar to what Barry said earlier. Was this why they were trying to start vampire hunts again? Why they were trying to show other vampires and humans that collaborating would lead to the ultimate hate crime, death?

Jareth leaned toward me, grabbing my attention again, his eyes dark as he examined me like a predator with his quarry.

"Don't you want to see how your power holds up to mine?" he asked softly in my ear. His voice trembled with excitement. I scooted my chair awkwardly away from him and took a long pull from my soda.

"No, thanks," I said after I swallowed. He busted up laughing as though I told the funniest joke he'd ever heard. Then again, I doubted most people joked with him. A heaviness fell over me, like gravity suddenly became a lot stronger and pulled me down. I dropped my fork and struggled to breathe.

"Fight back."

I looked at him but couldn't bring myself to do anything. What could I do against that? The pressure kept dragging me until I was on my knees. "Why?" I gasped out.

"Because it'll be fun."

What a psycho. I wanted to fight. I wanted him to eat his words and to wipe that stupid smirk off his face. But then the pull got stronger, and my face slammed into the floor.

Hale didn't show up in my   dreams. It felt like I was being abandoned. Almost sixteen meals had passed. Time meant nothing here. I could eat and read, but for the most part, I was just waiting to be summoned. My face was still swollen and covered in a dark purple bruise, and my arm was swollen to twice its size. Jareth must have broken something. Sure enough, the old necromancer walked through the door of my bedroom with a sickening grin.

"Time for you to learn to raise multiple people at once," he said and motioned for me to follow him. Maybe this *training* would help me get out of here. Or maybe I'd become as detached and cruel as they were. I thought back to my distressed zombie. I couldn't go through that again. If he tried to do that one more time, I'd really kill him.

"I'm surprised you're brave enough to see me again," I spat. I hated him. I really, truly hated him. And I wanted him to fear me.

"Well, we have a priest on standby this time, so I feel a bit more prepared. No one told me you could do that," he said with a chuckle as though he just learned I could juggle. What a freak. I glanced down at my arm and pressed a hand to my swollen cheek. Barry noticed and rolled his eyes. "If Jareth wants you healed, we'll have you healed."

He had me follow him down the hall, and this time, we stepped outside. There were twelve officers dead on the ground. All these people were in uniform, some with snapped necks and spines ripped out, others torn to pieces.

"Why were they killed?" I asked, but I already knew.

"The usual. They got too close. I think this was supposed to be your rescue team."

I nodded, but I didn't understand. These people in front of me were trying to save me. Barry, Jareth, the old man... they were monsters. Real-life monsters. The evil kind that wasn't capable of redemption.

"Want to bring them back to life?"

I glared at him. I knew. He wasn't trying to bring them back for good. No. He wanted me to raise them for his sick entertainment. These people would come back just to prove I could do it. Why couldn't they just rest in peace? My mind flashed to the basement where all those decaying carcasses were. Would they wind up there too? Piles of bodies beyond recognition?

Could I raise so many people at once? How would I do it? I looked at all the dead bodies. My totem twitched in my pocket. There was a hint of power in that totem. A hint of something much darker than me, even at my angriest. I could feel it calling to them. If I really wanted to, maybe my totem could help me raise them all. I stepped forward, and the scent of dried blood clung to my nose. Unfortunately, I was getting used to the smell. None of them looked at peace. Everyone had their eyes open and mouth agape, as though death took them by surprise.

Did I really want to force them back into this world?

"For someone that's meant to replace me, you're doing an awful job." His cackling echoed in the empty courtyard. Fine. I used the marble from my totem to slash my palm, then closed my hand into a fist and held it in front of me. I watched the blood drip onto the hard dirt.

There was a sense of power that surrounded us. Chilling to the bone, it called the dead. And they listened. I knew they did. These people wanted to know what I needed from them. The power I had willed them to do as I said.

"Come," I whispered, but my voice was firm.

Limbs reattached, cuts healed, and their eyes became full of a life they shouldn't possess. All twelve officers stood in a row and stared at me. They were waiting for orders.

"Outstanding. I knew you could do it," the old man said with a devilish grin. "Now let's see if you can keep hold of them."

I screamed "no" and reached out my hand just as his power jolted through me and through my zombies. Not again. I couldn't let him hurt my people a second time. One by one they started to convulse and shriek. So, I did the only thing I could think to do. I willed them to kill the old man. And they did.

All humanity was lost as they charged. A blond officer grabbed the old man and sank his teeth into his throat. I could see the look of panic on the necromancer's face, but I didn't care. Even as his emotions filled me with their fear and sorrow, I forced myself to ignore them. It wasn't until his face lost all sense of life that I allowed my zombies to go back to their former state. I didn't want them to regain consciousness and see what I made them do.

I made them murder a man. *I* murdered a man.

Chapter 23

I was going to die here. I stared at the dead necromancer at my feet and knew I was next. Jareth would kill me for this. The old man and I were going to be devoured by maggots like the others in the basement, and no one would be able to recognize our corpses. I didn't want to die like that. My knees collapsed on me, and I fell next to him. All the luxurious food I ate earlier looked like shit as I threw up on him.

I cried so hard, I choked on my own vomit. My throat burned as I struggled to breathe. Dammit. What did I do to deserve this?! I clung to whatever I could grab and dug my nails in. The old man's body squelched under me.

His essence shifted under my grip. I could bring him back to life with just a thought. I didn't want to. I hated the asshole. He had no respect for the dead and was such an arrogant dick. But he could help me. He knew the layout, right? Probably. But did I want someone so nasty to help me? My eyes were so blurry that I couldn't see what I was doing. But it didn't matter.

I needed him. I needed to get out of this hellish place. I could feel his life come back and I hated it. It was like a roach crawling on my skin. He moved out of the way gently so I could get my bearings while he stood. I was surprised he didn't try to help me up. More so that he wasn't shooting his decayed mouth off.

I wiped my eyes with my hands and my mouth with my sleeves. He was standing there with an expressionless face. He looked just like the zombies I'd raised before. Lifeless, but moving. It was exactly like I wanted him to be.

"Do you know the way out?" I croaked. He nodded and turned around to lead the way. Luckily, he didn't look that dead. His guts were no longer hanging out, which was a huge plus.

When we made it out to the hallway, I glanced at the cameras. "There's no way we're getting out unnoticed," I muttered. It didn't seem to be an issue though, because we didn't see anyone else as he led me through the building. It wasn't until we began passing hallways with windows that I could hear the gunshots.

"What's going on?" I asked and dropped to the ground to keep from getting shot. The old man stood above me and said nothing. It should have been creepy, but instead, it was comforting to see him so calm. I knew it was my doing. Every zombie I'd ever raised was just a person to me. But him? He was a monster. And monsters don't get to talk. I made him unable to talk. Ugh, that thought felt gross. I was just as bad as him. I didn't want to think that bastard rubbed off on me, but maybe he had.

The thud of a bullet hit him. My eyes widened, but he didn't even blink.

"Find her! She's the priority," a voice shouted. I stopped breathing. Rin. He was here.

"Rin!" I screamed. I meant to just call out to him. A casual *hey man, I'm over here.* But instead, I was full-on sobbing as I stumbled to my feet. "I'm here!"

Within moments, I was being held.

"Your face looks like shit. Why are you always getting into trouble?!" he hissed in my ear, but there was a raspy laugh with it. I shrugged my shoulders, although my right shoulder still hurt. My eyes burned. "You survived. Okay? You're alive. Let's get you home."

His group consisted of five men and three women, and each of them had a gun in their hands. They had to have silver bullets in there. I wasn't exactly expecting an introduction, but Rin was quick to motion them to secure the area. Not even eight seconds had passed before I knew something was wrong.

I felt them die before I heard Barry approach. All eight of the people Rin had with him were on the ground dead.

"Leaving? But I just started to like you."

My stomach twisted. He was going to kill Rin. I was going to be stuck here. Dizziness. Standing felt hard. But it couldn't end like this. Rin. I had to protect him.

Rin was trembling with a mixture of rage, horror, and sadness from beside me. I had no idea how close his people were to him, but Barry had killed them in less than a minute. They didn't have a chance.

I glared at Barry and held out my hands, my totem held between my pointer and middle finger. I thought about all the murder victims. The gardener, the warehouse workers, the churchgoers, and the cafe girls. I had to watch them relive him killing them. Each of them had to relive watching him kill someone they knew and then dying themselves. They all acted so tough, but none of them deserved to die. He killed them. Why?! But at that moment, I stopped caring about the reason.

I needed every ounce of my power. I glanced at the old man, and he stood beside me too. His power of necromancy had no master. He was dead. So, I took it from him. The power I stole became part of me. Borrowed power. Didn't matter. I let its icy breath wash over me. It felt like hours, but I knew it had only been seconds. I needed Barry to die, which meant I needed to do what I did best. The dead rose. Not just Rin's people, but the staked vampires on the ground too. Barry stared at me. There was no hint of surprise. Just hate. Loathing.

"This is why I said he should kill you," he growled.

I nodded.

"Yeah, he probably should have."

It was an adrenaline rush. Controlling vampires was unheard of. I was just a human. Yet here I was, a master of the undead. I remembered just a few days ago thinking I was so easy to kill. But now, I had power. This was real power. The totem twitched in my hand.

They lunged. It was a mesh of zombies and vampires. Teeth bared. Hands with unnatural strength. He threw two zombies off at the same time. Three vampires grabbed him from behind. They bit him. The way he howled made me cringe. But I had to watch. I needed to see them rip him apart. Strips of flesh. His arm lay on the ground. His clothes a bloody mess. But his eyes. They never stopped looking at me.

We both knew. I was killing him.

"Lily, what-," Rin started. I shook my head. Barry's head fell at my feet.

"Think we can bring this to Malik?" I asked with a forced smile.

Chapter 24

The police arrived. There weren't a lot of people alive, but the ones who were were arrested. Except for me and Rin. We managed to get blankets and hot chocolate. Well, I got hot chocolate. Rin asked for coffee instead.

"So, you don't know why the vampires turned on our suspect?" Malik asked with an eyebrow raised.

"Nope. Vampires are so funny that way. They just do things, super crazy things," I said with a smile. It was still hard to believe I managed to raise vampires from the dead. That was supposed to be impossible. But as soon as they finished killing Barry, the raised vampires went back to being dead. Outside of Rin and I, there were no other witnesses. Rin already told me that Hale's people deleted the surveillance footage. I guess I was grateful. What if the police had seen me kill the old necromancer? What if they saw I could raise vampires? I didn't want Malik to see me that way. Like I really was a monster.

"Fine," Malik said, his eyes cold. I tried to ignore his probing stare. I had nothing to say to him. Rin patted my knee, which caught Malik's eye. "I'm guessing you will stick with your bodyguard instead of police protection."

"Yeah," Rin said with an eye roll.

"I understand. I would be wary too given your circumstances. Outside of the Church of Eternal Life, it appears as though you're mostly safe. I will put you on leave for the next two weeks." He turned and walked away toward the flashing lights and people in uniform. It was so surreal. I was free. I also really wanted to read the next book in My Undead Romance. Servant girl, whatever her name was, had really, really good taste in books.

I watched the medical personnel walk past carrying gurney after gurney. They were going to need to make a few trips to get everyone to the morgue.

"Are you listening?"

I nodded, but if Rin had been talking, I hadn't heard shit. With so many dead bodies it'd probably take a while to hold that many funerals. The people in the basement... would they be able to be identified? I guessed dental records. Yeah, most people went to the dentist at some point. Somebody would find their dead person.

"Lily, you're crying."

I touched my face to verify the wetness. Yeah, I really was crying.

"If Hale dies, do you think there'll still be a body? Jareth won't completely destroy him, right?"

Rin grabbed my face and forced me to look at him.

"Listen to me very carefully. Can you do that?"

I nodded, but I wasn't sure how accurate that was. I was distracted by a nonstop flood of thoughts about everything I did. Even now, I could feel my totem in my pocket. If I wanted to, I could raise them all. Apparently, that meant the vampires too. I could bring everyone back for goodbyes. I could bring them back to fight. Or I could bring them back lifeless.

"Jareth is done."

That caught my attention.

"Hale killed him?"

"No. But his top people are dead. It's over. When we came to get you, the facility had his top men there. A bunch were taken in by the cops and then you killed Jareth's right hand. He doesn't have his elite forces anymore."

I shook my head repeatedly. Even when I became dizzy, I kept shaking my head. Jareth wouldn't stop.

I couldn't talk anymore, and after falling asleep sitting up twice, Malik let Rin take me home.

I fell asleep and prayed I wouldn't have another dream alone. Hale, where were you?

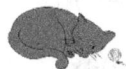

Hale wasn't in my dream. Even in my sleep, I searched for him. I woke up in the middle of the night, partially out of frustration, but also because the air felt surprisingly still and dead. I glanced around the room and found Rin sleeping on the ground next to me on his side. Within moments, his eyes were open, and he was sitting up.

"You okay?"

I blinked in surprise, not expecting him to jump to attention over me waking up in the middle of the night. I opened my mouth to respond, but then his eyes narrowed and he covered my mouth with his hand. I could tell by the intensity of his gaze as he looked at the bedroom door that something was wrong.

"Jareth is here." He breathed the words so quietly, I almost missed them.

My eyes widened, and I clung to him, but he just shook his head at me. How did he know?! And yet, in that moment, I reached out with my powers, searching for the dead. I could feel him, and it burned like ice that you kept against your skin for too long. I quickly retracted my powers.

"Lily, you have to survive. No matter what happens, do what you can to make it," Rin told me quietly, his voice so firm I flinched.

I scrambled to stand up, but he was already moving in the darkness towards the bedroom door.

"Little priestess, where are you?" Jareth's voice crooned from the other room. Chills ran down my spine. That voice. I never wanted to hear it again.

"I'm afraid we're going to have to speed things up. Where. Are. You?" he asked, his voice darker now.

The door to the bedroom burst open. Rin had a gun in his hand and aimed to shoot. He must have had silver bullets. Silver does shit to Master Vampires.

Rin fired until the gun ran out of bullets, every single one of them missing Jareth. He was too fast. My eyes widened as Jareth's fingers wrapped around Rin's throat.

"Don't kill him!" I screamed so loud my throat burned and my eyes watered. I saw it. It was only for an instant, but Jareth hesitated. Rin's eyes widened as he looked at me, but then Jareth threw him into a wall.

"I'll let it pass for now. We don't have time, after all," Jareth smiled, but I could feel it. He was playing it off, but I really controlled him. At that moment, I made a Master Vampire obey my will.

He grabbed hold of me. I tried to protest but that was enough for him to shove a gag in my mouth. "Not now, little priestess," he murmured and held a hand over my eyes.

Chapter 25

When I opened my eyes, I was in a cemetery. It was a dream. I could tell because the graves smelled fresh, the bodies felt absent, and the moon was a bit too bright. Beautiful ambiance, but not reality. He was here somewhere. Sure enough, Hale stepped out from a mausoleum and sauntered towards me.

Hale looked more tired than I'd ever seen him. His hair was limp and oily, his eyes dark, and he seemed thinner. I didn't think vampires could get smaller. He reached out slowly and took me in his arms. Just like Rin, he seemed grateful to see me. Did they think I was going to die? I guess I thought that too for a while.

"What happened?" I asked. "Is Rin alive?" Gods. If he died because of me... I stopped breathing.

Hale laughed bitterly; his icy breath tickled my neck. Did vampires breathe? Maybe in dreams.

"I thought if enough of his people were killed or taken in, he'd leave to regroup. Naive. I didn't realize he would take you with him," Hale explained, his voice detached, as though he was lost in his thoughts. "Rin's alive. It was only a concussion. He should be grateful he's breathing, even though he failed."

Hale's tone became dark. It sounded like he was furious, maybe even like he might kill Rin for "failing." But he couldn't. Rin did the best he could to protect me and nearly died trying. He shouldn't be punished for that!

"He was against Jareth. What do you mean 'failed'?" I demanded. I was angry. My whole body was trembling. No one could go against Jareth. How dare he imply Rin did something wrong?!

He pulled back and looked at me then. His eyes bore into mine as though searching for something.

"You're right. It's not like last time. Jareth kidnapped you personally."

"Why?"

"He's fleeing, and I guess he decided you're worth taking with."

I thought back to all the training. It made some kind of sick sense. He put time and effort into making me get stronger. But he just lost his followers and Barry. What was I compared to that?

"All he has left," I sighed.

"What?"

"He wanted me to learn how to be stronger. He specifically had me train my necromancy while I was with him. I think he wanted something more once he found out what I could do," I said way too quickly. I stumbled over my words as I tried to sort it out in my head. What could someone do with a necromancer?

I was stupid. I knew. Even when I tried not to, I could still remember those officers ripping the old man to shreds while I watched. He could have me do that on a much greater scale. There was more too. He saw how my empathy could be used as a weapon.

"You'll be his new right hand," Hale said slowly.

"But, I don't like him," I protested.

"You wouldn't have to. He just needs to have some kind of leverage over you. And unfortunately," he said this with such sorrow in his voice, I teared up, "you're such a good person. It's easy to hold something over someone kind. You just have to threaten to be mean."

I wanted to argue, to tell him this was all some kind of mistake. There was no way. I was just an intern. I only recently started raising humans from the dead. There was no way someone that powerful and evil wanted me.

"Lily, I'm going to find you. I'm not strong enough to kill Jareth, but I promise, I'll save you."

I wanted to believe him. Our lips meshed together in a desperate mess, and I wondered, not for the first time, if I was going to die.

Chapter 26

I woke up in the middle of a field on an air tarmac, slung across someone's shoulders. I started to kick and push at the person, making him dump me to the ground, scraping my knees on the asphalt. It was burning hot. I flinched as I quickly hopped to my feet.

I looked at Jareth in horror. He was just walking along the tarmac in the sunlight. How was a vampire doing that?! He turned back to me and gave me a lazy smile.

"Morning, my little priestess. Did you sleep well?" he asked, his tone deceptively warm despite him dropping my ass on the ground a moment ago. He was wearing tight black leather pants and a bright yellow jacket, which was zipped up.

I turned to run, but he was behind me in seconds, his arm wrapped around my waist while his other hand grabbed mine. My arm was still swollen from the last time he grabbed it, and I was already closing my eyes, waiting for the same pain to envelop my hand, but this time, he was gentle.

"Be a good girl for me," he said as he released me.

"How are you in the sunlight?" I demanded as I tried to reach out with my powers. I wanted to destroy Jareth or control him or do *anything*. But nothing happened, and he just smiled at me like I was a cute and innocent little *thing*.

"Master Vampires have special tricks. Did your precious Hale not tell you?" Jareth's cold hand patted me on the head, and I flinched. If I could, I would hit him right now and force him under my control like I did back at the apartment. But all the energy I kept putting into staring him down and trying to reach out with my powers did *nothing*. I had no idea how I did it back then, and he still threw Rin against a wall. My breath came back. Rin was alive though. At least I didn't get him killed.

"What are you going to do with me?" I asked, my tone dripping in amusement. My entire body felt stiff from fear, but I could fake confidence. I'd had plenty of practice. Being scared shitless was becoming too common. Right now, I needed to stall. Someone would find me. Just stall.

"Then you might have to enjoy the plane ride unconscious," Jareth said with a shrug and released me. He ran his fingers through his hair and smiled wryly at me.

I looked past him and saw it, the plane. My blood ran cold. It was a small sky-blue plane with what looked like missiles at the end of each wing. The tail was shaped like an upside-down T. There was glass encasing the cockpit, so I could see the two-seat setup and the interior, which matched Jareth's current attire, black lining with a yellow plush finish.

Why was the scariest man I ever met in my life simultaneously an absolute dork?

And yet, this was a plane. A motherfucking airplane. We could go anywhere in this. I wouldn't be coming back. I thought about Hale and Rin. Mint. Jazz and Amy. I was getting further and further from my home.

"I did some research on you, Miss Lily Clarke," Jareth said casually, as though there was anything to know about me. "Did you know you're the youngest person to ever become a necromancer? Necromancy beginning at age eight is unheard of. Normally it manifests in a human's twenties or thirties if ever at all. And yet, you managed to become one so young."

Why was he telling me this? For a moment, I thought back to the interrogation room with Malik. He also brought up the age when I became a necromancer. Why were people so interested?

Jareth pulled me toward the plane, our steps leisurely, as though we had all the time in the world.

I said nothing. What could I say? I mean, I knew I was young when I found out I was a necromancer, but I didn't really think anything of it. It caused problems for me, sure. My mom tried to get me to stop raising the dead, not like it worked. But if that was really so unique, then...

"Did you know you disappeared for two years?" he continued without looking at me. I froze. What? "That was a particularly interesting tidbit. I only found out because of a witch. It took her three days to get past that particular spell. After that, you were suddenly a necromancer. Interesting coincidence, isn't it? You were gone and no one remembered you, then you came back and raised a piece of human roadkill from the dead."

My blood ran cold as I tried to process what he was telling me. I mean, yeah, I didn't remember how the whole necromancy thing started. I just... could do it. Did I remember kindergarten? First grade? The more I thought about it, the less I felt I knew. Was it normal for people to remember that stuff? Did something happen to me? Malik had also mentioned I raised a human from the dead back then. That my first zombie was a friend of mine. NOT roadkill. I opened my mouth to ask more, but then he released me abruptly.

Five armored black cars raced up to us and stopped abruptly, causing dirt to fly into the air like a cloud. Within moments, a shot came from one of the cars, and I dropped to the ground instinctively. I'd never been around guns this much before.

I heard a *splish* as brains and blood dripped over my shoulders. I looked up in horror at the gaping hole where Jareth's face had been. I stumbled to my feet and checked my surroundings, and yet, I realized Jareth's body wasn't dropping. Instead, his face was reconstructing. I covered my mouth with my hands and scrambled backwards, trying to get away from him. Jareth took the last few steps to the plane and hopped in without me, and I nearly cried. I could hear my name and saw Rin and Hale standing next to one of the armored cars while SWAT got out swiftly and aimed their guns at the plane. Seeing Hale in the sunlight told me Jareth wasn't lying. I guess it really was a Master Vampire thing.

Jareth was already starting up the plane casually, as though he had no reason to rush, and gave a wave. But his gaze. He was staring at me so intensely that I felt dizzy. Hale wrapped his arms around me, pulling me close, and I noticed Detective Malik shouting orders I couldn't hear while the plane began to move.

Jareth was going to get away.

"I'm here, you're not going anywhere," Hale said. He looked so much more beautiful in real life than in my dreams. I felt like I was about to lose consciousness as I clung to him. When was the last time I ate? So much adrenaline all this time. Was I crashing? Tears filled my eyes. No. I had to stay awake.

I watched the plane fly away and heard people talking.

"Lily, we're going to have to ask some questions." Malik's voice sounded tired. I could feel it too. Everyone was so exhausted and done with the situation.

"Okay," I said but didn't move. Hale had to help me get to a nearby car. I made them keep him with me, so he sat next to me while they asked questions. I couldn't answer much. Just that Jareth and his men had me raise zombies for them and he was going to take me with him somewhere. Malik tried to sound sympathetic, but the frustration was there.

After about an hour, they let me go. I think they could tell I was practically a walking corpse. To my surprise, Hale stayed with me. Rin didn't follow us to the loft; he seemed fine but said he needed a break. I guess I was too much for him.

Hale and I shared the bed but didn't kiss or have sex. It was a comfort thing, and it worked. For the first time in a long time, I felt safe.

Chapter 27

My phone had several missed calls from Jazz.

"Where've you been? I've been holding onto Mint and this other stupid cat for you for like a week," they complained. My eyes widened.

"You found Aphrodite?!"

"One of my viewers found her downtown and let me know. I picked her up, and she's just been waiting here for you. When are you coming by?"

I glanced at Hale, who just smiled, so I took that as a go ahead.

"I'll swing by today."

When I got Aphrodite safely into Hale's BMW, I called Mrs. Bennett. I guess she must have saved my number, because instead of her butler, she answered directly.

"Yes, what is it?"

"I have your cat."

"Oh. My. Gods. Did you really find my baby? When are you bringing her? Can it be now? I'll pay you more if you bring her now."

Well shit, then, yeah, we're gonna go right now. Rin was our bodyguard and driver. I tried to talk to Rin, to joke with him, but Rin stopped talking. He acknowledged I was there, but that was it. Hale seemed amused but said nothing about the situation. He treated Rin like a personal driver, no personable relations between the two. It was so weird, and that newfound coldness made me so lonely. I lost my friend, and I had no idea why.

"So, you've raised two people from the dead trying to find this cat?"

"Yup, and almost killed a catnapper too."

"And this is how you began working for the police?" he asked incredulously.

"Yup, my first human raising was someone Barry killed who also worked for her. The dead guy took the cat to the groomer before he died," I explained with a shrug. I tried to make this as toned down as I could, but it really was incredible. In just a couple weeks, my world had completely changed.

When we pulled up, Mrs. Bennett was outside. She didn't wait for the car to stop and rushed forward. She pulled at the handle three times trying to get to her cat. Rin rolled his eyes and unlocked the door for her.

She threw open the door of the cat crate and held her cat in her arms. Despite not having a groomer for a couple of weeks, Aphrodite still looked like a fluffy white cat with a clean and soft coat. Mrs. Bennett kissed her over and over again while sobbing. The cat didn't seem to care either way and just let out a drawling meow.

"I have a sorcerer here to put a tracker on you, baby. I'll never lose you again!"

"I don't mean to be nosy, but did you find out who was behind the attempted assassination of your cat? You had said something about your boyfriend before. Was it him?" I asked as I slowly got out of the car. Hale and Rin followed me out silently. It felt like overkill, but I didn't mind being looked after. It was better than being kidnapped again.

"Oh that," she laughed and waved it off. "My boyfriend, Harold, just got a little jealous. We've talked about it, and he won't try to kill her anymore. He just won't be coming to her monthly tea party." Monthly tea party? For a cat? "Oh, it's a catnip blend. She and her other kitty friends absolutely love it!" I guess she noticed my disbelief.

"But doesn't that mean he killed Alejandra, your chef?!" I normally don't shout at clients, but holy fuck. That lady was sweet as hell, and Mrs. Bennett didn't care at all that her beau was a murderer!

"Well, the police didn't charge him or even suspect him, so how should I know who murdered her?" The lack of compassion in her voice made my blood boil, but I needed the money, and it's not like I could go arrest the guy. But I would definitely be giving Malik more info about this. There's no guarantee the guy won't try to kill me again later. Mrs. Bennett held the cat tighter and motioned for us to follow her inside. It didn't seem like she'd be letting Aphrodite down anytime soon, even when the cat squirmed in her grip.

Her house was large, too large. I'd get lost trying to make my way through the courtyard. The inside was probably the same, but her office was by the front door, so we didn't have to go too far to get to her checkbook. "I don't remember exactly what we said, but I believe this is about that number," she said and handed me a check for twenty thousand. I couldn't help it. Tears filled my eyes and my throat closed up. "If this is good enough, then please leave. I have much I need to do for my princess' return." Despite the abruptness, she still hugged me goodbye before a maid led us to the car.

"So, what's next?" Hale asked and kissed me. Rin looked away and focused on getting the car in gear. He'd become much quieter since I got back.

"I don't know," I whispered. I got that job done. Undead, Inc., had tried to fire me for going AWOL, but since I had the police report proving I was kidnapped, the firing was retracted. And now I had enough money to pay my ex-roommates back, plus take some college classes for my bachelor's degree. It felt like my world was complete, finally. I wasn't able to control vampires anymore, and raising more than one human at a time was next to impossible for me. I tried to test it out on a couple vampires Hale brought me and then with humans in a graveyard one night, but it just never worked. It must have been a fluke back at Jareth's compound. It seemed like my whole existence had been drained. So whatever superpowers I had when I was with Jareth seemed to be gone for now. Good riddance. That was scary as hell.

"Would you do me the honor of going on a date with me?" Hale asked, his eyes brightening as I slowly nodded.

The date was simple. He reserved seats at a sushi restaurant and watched me eat. It was weird and definitely gave off Jareth vibes, but the conversation was nice.

"Are we living together from now on?" I asked, and he smiled.

"No."

"But I can still stay where I'm at?"

"Of course. I just ask that you raise at least one person for me a month. If you can do that, then your room will be paid for."

"Who will I be raising?"

"Celebrities mostly. I have people I'd like to impress," he said with no hesitation. So, was he going to use my abilities as a bribe?

"You admitted that so easily," I laughed nervously.

"Few people have done as much for me as you have. I see no reason to be dishonest in our relationship."

I was reminded once again how princely he was. And as much as I wanted to believe in his charm, I knew he now controlled the entire DFW area. Other humans may not have known it, but every vampire in the area had to answer to him. This wasn't the kind of relationship I could take lightly. But then he smiled, and I melted.

"I'd like to make these dinners recurring, and not just for business. I'd like to date you," he said, and I could feel his nervous sincerity. How could I possibly doubt someone like this?

So, against my better judgment, I decided to date a vampire.

About the Author

Lily Clemons has been writing since she was five years old. At the time, she thought she needed to learn how to chop down trees in order to make her novels, but luckily, she was introduced to office supply stores. An avid fan of monster-of-the-week shows and novels, she was inspired to create her own. Lily has a bachelor's degree in communications as well as English with a certification in technical writing all from the University of North Texas. She has a ten-year-old fashionista and a husband who supplies hugs, alone time, and helpful reminders like the fact that food exists. This is the first of many to come, so please enjoy the journey!

Check out the website, the newsletter, and more with the QR below!

The sequel, *Succubi's Consent* will be coming soon...

www.ingramcontent.com/pod-product-compliance
Lightning Source LLC
Chambersburg PA
CBHW071323250626
47159CB00004B/1440